"Why Did You Kiss Me That Way?" She Demanded.

"That way?" Seth asked. "Well, that particular kiss—number seven—just happens to be the best way I know how," he quipped.

She didn't alter her expression. "But *why* did you do it?"

"Why did you let me?"

She shook her head. "Don't ever do that again."

Seth inhaled a slow, steadying breath. "Then tell me, Prudence, what *do* you want? I seem to recall something of a personal nature that you needed to discuss with me—*alone*."

"I want you…" Her voice trailed off.

Hope flickered inside Seth. "You want me?"

He arched an eyebrow quizzically.

"I mean—" She inhaled one more breath, and released it in a rush of words. "I want you—need you—to be my husband."

Dear Reader,

Twenty years ago in May, the first Silhouette romance was published, and in 2000 we're celebrating our 20th anniversary all year long! Celebrate with us—and start with six powerful, passionate, provocative love stories from Silhouette Desire.

Elizabeth Bevarly offers a MAN OF THE MONTH so tempting that we decided to call it *Dr. Irresistible!* Enjoy this sexy tale about a single-mom nurse who enlists a handsome doctor to pose as her husband at her tenth high school reunion. The wonderful miniseries LONE STAR FAMILIES: THE LOGANS, by bestselling author Leanne Banks, continues with *Expecting His Child,* a sensual romance about a woman carrying the child of her family's nemesis after a stolen night of passion.

Ever-talented Cindy Gerard returns to Desire with *In His Loving Arms,* in which a pregnant widow is reunited with the man who's haunted her dreams for seven years. Sheikhs abound in Alexandra Sellers' *Sheikh's Honor,* a new addition to her dramatic miniseries SONS OF THE DESERT. The Desire theme promotion, THE BABY BANK, about women who find love unexpectedly when seeking sperm donors, continues with Metsy Hingle's *The Baby Bonus.* And newcomer Kathie DeNosky makes her Desire debut with *Did You Say Married?!,* in which the heroine wakes up in Vegas next to a sexy cowboy who turns out to be her newly wed husband.

What a lineup! So this May, for Mother's Day, why not treat your mom—and yourself—to all six of these highly sensual and emotional love stories from Silhouette Desire!

Enjoy!

Joan Marlow Golan

Joan Marlow Golan
Senior Editor, Silhouette Desire

Please address questions and book requests to:
Silhouette Reader Service
U.S.: 3010 Walden Ave., P.O. Box 1325, Buffalo, NY 14269
Canadian: P.O. Box 609, Fort Erie, Ont. L2A 5X3

Dr. Irresistible
ELIZABETH BEVARLY

~Silhouette®

Desire

Published by Silhouette Books
America's Publisher of Contemporary Romance

For Eli,
my little guy,
who is truly irresistible.

SILHOUETTE BOOKS

ISBN 0-373-76291-7

DR. IRRESISTIBLE

Copyright © 2000 by Elizabeth Bevarly

Visit Silhouette at www.eHarlequin.com

Printed in U.S.A.

Books by Elizabeth Bevarly

Silhouette Desire

An Unsuitable Man for the Job #724
Jake's Christmas #753
A Lawless Man #856
*A Dad Like Daniel #908
*The Perfect Father #920
*Dr. Daddy #933
†Father of the Brat #993
†Father of the Brood #1005
†Father on the Brink #1016
‡Roxy and the Rich Man #1053
‡Lucy and the Loner #1063
‡Georgia Meets Her Groom #1083
**Bride of the Bad Boy #1124
**Beauty and the Brain #1130
**The Virgin and the Vagabond #1136
The Sheriff and the Impostor Bride #1184
††Society Bride #1196
That Boss of Mine #1231
*A Doctor in Her Stocking #1252
*Dr. Mommy #1269
*Dr. Irresistible #1291

Silhouette Special Edition

Destinations South #557
Close Range #590
Donovan's Chance #639
Moriah's Mutiny #676
Up Close #737
Hired Hand #803
Return Engagement #844

*From Here to Maternity
†From Here to Paternity
‡The Family McCormick
**Blame It on Bob
††Fortune's Children:
    The Brides

ELIZABETH BEVARLY

is an honors graduate of the University of Louisville and achieved her dream of writing full-time before she even turned thirty! At heart, she is also an avid voyager who once helped navigate a friend's thirty-five-foot sailboat across the Bermuda Triangle. Her dream is to one day have her own sailboat, a beautifully renovated older-model forty-two-footer, and to enjoy the freedom and tranquillity seafaring can bring. Elizabeth likes to think she has a lot in common with the characters she creates, people who know love and life go hand in hand. And she's getting some firsthand experience with motherhood, as well—she and her husband have a six-year-old son, Eli.

IT'S OUR 20th ANNIVERSARY!
We'll be celebrating all year,
Continuing with these fabulous titles,
On sale in May 2000.

Romance

 #1444 Mercenary's Woman
Diana Palmer

#1445 Too Hard To Handle
Rita Rainville

 #1446 A Royal Mission
Elizabeth August

#1447 Tall, Strong & Cool Under Fire
Marie Ferrarella

 #1448 Hannah Gets a Husband
Julianna Morris

#1449 Her Sister's Child
Lilian Darcy

Desire

 #1291 Dr. Irresistible
Elizabeth Bevarly

 #1292 Expecting His Child
Leanne Banks

#1293 In His Loving Arms
Cindy Gerard

 #1294 Sheikh's Honor
Alexandra Sellers

 #1295 The Baby Bonus
Metsy Hingle

#1296 Did You Say Married?!
Kathie DeNosky

Intimate Moments

 #1003 Rogue's Reform
Marilyn Pappano

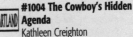 **#1004 The Cowboy's Hidden Agenda**
Kathleen Creighton

#1005 In a Heartbeat
Carla Cassidy

 #1006 Anything for Her Marriage
Karen Templeton

#1007 Every Little Thing
Linda Winstead Jones

 #1008 Remember the Night
Linda Castillo

Special Edition

#1321 The Kincaid Bride
Jackie Merritt

 #1322 The Millionaire She Married
Christine Rimmer

#1323 Warrior's Embrace
Peggy Webb

#1324 The Sheik's Arranged Marriage
Susan Mallery

#1325 Sullivan's Child
Gail Link

#1326 Wild Mustang
Jane Toombs

One

Dr. Seth Mahoney fingered the scalpel in his left hand gingerly, wondering where, exactly, to begin the incision he needed to make. The nurse standing beside him, who gazed over his shoulder, likewise pondered the heart that lay waiting for cutting, but she said nothing to inspire Seth's decision. It was a tricky business, how to proceed, and there was an enormous amount of pressure on him to do this correctly. The happiness of more than a few people depended on the success of this operation.

For long moments he pondered his dilemma. Should he cut straight up and down? Or across the middle? Diagonally? If so, which way? From left auricle to right ventricle? Or from left ventricle to right auricle? And which ones were the auricles, anyway? Top or bottom? He always had gotten auricles and ventricles confused. And how many pieces was he supposed to cut the heart into again? He'd forgotten.

Finally, unable to decide how best to perform this particular procedure and, quite frankly, at his wit's end, Seth muttered, "Ah, what the hell." Then he curled his fist around the scalpel's handle and, with one fierce jab, drove it deep into the center of the heart.

"Oh, nicely done, Dr. Mahoney," the nurse beside him muttered wryly. "I bet you're the kind of guy who runs with scissors, too, aren't you?"

"Hey, cut me some slack, Renee," he countered, spinning around to face her full-on. With much exasperation, he ran both hands through his pale-blond hair, then doubled them into fists on his Dockers-clad hips. "You act like this is such a big deal. I mean, jeez, it's not brain surgery, you know."

And of course he himself *did* know. He was one of New Jersey's—hey, perhaps one of the nation's—leading neurosurgeons. He just didn't know squat about hearts, that was all.

Especially hearts made of cake.

"Congratulations on your engagement, Renee," he muttered to the room at large. He left the scalpel where it lay, jutting garishly out of the blood-red icing. "I'm just so damned happy for you, I can't stand it. Nor can I cut this cake. You guys are on your own."

Hell, let everybody cut their own pieces, he thought. How was he supposed to get two dozen slices of equal size from such a strangely shaped confection, anyway? "Some of us have pulled double duty and would like to go home," he continued irritably. "Now if you'll excuse me…?"

As an afterthought he withdrew the scalpel, intent on returning it to the OR, from which he'd filched it in the first place. But before he could even complete one step toward the exit, the entreaties began in earnest.

"Oh, come on, Dr. Mahoney," a collection of voices

cajoled. Nurses, doctors and orderlies alike begged his forgiveness and urged him to stay.

"We're sorry, Seth…"

"We didn't mean it…"

"We were just kidding…"

"We'll let you have the biggest piece…"

"You're the only one who knows how to do this right…"

"We need that scalpel—we couldn't find a knife…"

But their gentle wheedling did little to soothe him. He was tired, he was irritable, he'd had a rotten day and he wanted to go home. The last thing he wanted to do was join his colleagues in a party to celebrate the upcoming marriage of one of their own. It was just too fitting a Friday punctuation mark for what had been a lousy week.

Nothing had seemed to go right today. Nothing. His BMW roadster had made funny noises all the way to work this morning, and he—*he*, Dr. Seth Mahoney, ace mechanic—couldn't for the life of him figure out what was wrong with it. He'd been drenched by rain as he'd sprinted from the parking lot to the hospital, because he—*he*, Dr. Seth Mahoney, mind like a steel trap—had forgotten his umbrella. And as he'd changed into his scrubs, he'd realized that he—*he*, Dr. Seth Mahoney, sartorial wonder—was wearing one black sock and one gray sock.

Fortunately Mrs. Hammelman's surgery had gone well. He was, after all, one of New Jersey's—hey, perhaps one of the nation's—leading neurosurgeons. But everything else that day had been a mess. The cafeteria had been out of club sandwiches by the time he'd found a minute to grab lunch. The soda machine had been out of Orange Crush when he'd gone on a break. Then the ATM in the lobby had told him that he—*he*, Dr. Seth Mahoney, financial wizard—was overdrawn a full $3.86. And he'd had a pounding headache for the past three hours that simply would not be assuaged.

And to top it all off it was Friday, and he—*he,* Dr. Seth Mahoney, object of many a woman's desire—did *not* have a date.

He didn't have a *date,* he marveled for perhaps the hundredth time. How on earth could such a thing have happened?

By now he'd had enough of the hospital and its denizens, and he wanted to go home. Home, where he could kick off his shoes, and his mismatched socks, fix himself a club sandwich—which would be better than the hospital's, anyway—open an Orange Crush, and call the bank to yell at someone about his ridiculous, and certainly nonexistent, overdraft.

Of course, the date part was going to be something of a problem, he mused sullenly. He couldn't think of anyone else to ask out—no one who would say yes, at any rate— and he wasn't much for inflatable women. Then again, the way today had been going, he was sorely tempted to—

The thought never fully materialized in his brain, thanks to the woman who breezed into the room just then. He couldn't quite curb the soft smile he felt curling his lips when he noted her arrival. Prudence Holloway, the most bewitching, bothering and bewildering woman he had ever had the dubious good fortune to encounter. And the most inappropriately named, too, he recalled, his smile growing broader.

Prudence, he thought. What *had* her parents been thinking?

Well, well, well. Maybe he didn't have to beat such a hasty retreat just yet.

"Hi, everybody," she said breathlessly to the room at large.

She raked a restive hand through the mop of dark-auburn

curls that danced atop her head with the rush of her movements. Although he had always been partial to long hair on women, somehow Seth was grateful that Prudence's unruly tresses weren't quite lengthy enough to cover her nape. She had a nice neck. Among other things.

Inescapably, his gaze fell to the top half of the shapeless, raspberry-colored nurse's scrubs. Although he had no foundation for his suspicions—God knew Prudence wouldn't let him get within arm's reach of her, more's the pity—he was fairly certain that the baggy garment hid some truly spectacular and decidedly dangerous curves.

The only time he'd seen her *out* of her scrubs, she'd been *in* something else—more's the pity—namely maternity clothes, generally made out of some awful awning-like fabric and decorated with bows and frippery that no self-respecting woman would dare don when she was unpregnant. Prudence had been huge, unwieldy and irascible during her pregnancy, Seth recalled wistfully. And during that entire nine-month span, he'd been even more enchanted by her than ever. Because Prudence Holloway was just too adorable to ever be anything but…well…adorable.

Ever since he'd come to work at Seton General Hospital two years ago, Seth had been utterly enraptured by Nurse Prudence Holloway. Why? He had no idea. Maybe because her pale-green eyes were so expressive and held no secrets. Maybe because her lush mouth, whether smiling or frowning, open or closed, could incite a man to commit mayhem. Maybe because he had noticed right off that she had a wry sense of humor and quick wit. Maybe because she had been so huge and irascible during her pregnancy. He hated to say it, but she was just so damned cute when she was angry.

Or maybe it was just because, even when she wasn't pregnant, she continued to be, if not huge, then certainly irascible. At least around Seth. And he simply was not accustomed to having women respond to him in a way that was anything but enraptured. Even complete strangers succumbed to his abundant charm. Prudence, however, had been anything *but* charmed by him. Even after two years, her resolve to avoid and deter him had eroded not one iota.

Two years ago Seth had assured himself that her less-than-eager response to his more-than-obvious allure had resulted from the fact that she was seeing someone. She'd been blinded—who knows why, when she could have had Seth?—by some geek named Kevin who had worked as a pump jockey in a less-than-profitable filling station.

And then, after that relationship had fizzled, and Prudence continued to avoid Seth, he had excused her disinterest in his none-too-subtle advances as being due to her delicate condition. Because she was out of sorts and uncomfortable in her pregnant state, and romance was understandably the last thing on her mind. He'd even thought her lack of response might be because she was still carrying a torch for that geek Kevin—though such a commitment to a man hadn't kept other women from succumbing to Seth before. On many occasions.

Not that he would *ever* pursue a married woman, of course. He simply never felt hindered in his flirtations by a woman's marital state. Or her background. Or her foreground. Or her middle ground. Or her age, race, creed, color, species or planetary origin. And he saw no harm in engaging in the occasional flip comment whenever there was a beautiful woman around.

And naturally, to Seth, *all* women fell into that beautiful category. And he—*he,* Dr. Seth Mahoney, lover of women—was simply predisposed to flirting with anything that produced estrogen. Prudence Holloway was no exception.

Except…

Except that Seth couldn't seem to *stop* flirting with her, even though she'd made it more than clear over the past two years that she did *not* intend to indulge his efforts. And that was something he simply could not understand. Because, simply put, there was no *Mr.* Prudence Holloway. Nor did there seem to be a Mr. Prudence Holloway in training anywhere. And her obviously—and adamantly—single status was something that only fueled Seth's, oh…idle curiosity about the nurse.

And it had naturally caused him to pump up the volume on his flirtations, too. He'd even ventured to ask her out once or twice—or fifty-seven times, but then, who was counting? But she'd always declined. Politely at first, then with more gusto. He supposed it had been the time he'd dropped onto his knees before her in the OR and begged her to go out with him that had promoted the gusto on her part, but still…

The least she could do was return his flirtations, even if she had no interest in carrying through with them. Hey, any other nurse would do the same. It was only polite. But not Prudence. Noooo. She constantly rebuffed him.

Him. Dr. Seth Mahoney. Dr. Irresistible.

How could she *do* such a thing?

In the long run Seth had finally given up asking her out, when it became clear that she would never, ever, not in a million billion trillion *zillion* years, not if he was the last man on the planet, dead *or* alive, go out with him. He knew that, because she'd told him that. In exactly those words. And the fact that he—*he,* Dr. Seth Mahoney, a prince among men—had failed in his quest to curry fair Prudence's favor did not sit well with him at all.

Still, he no longer asked her out. But he hadn't stopped his entirely one-sided and unreturned flirting. Nor had he stopped fantasizing about her during his off hours. Or during his on hours, for that matter. Like right now, for instance. As his thoughts drifted off to the sublime, Prudence tossed a Tupperware container full of what appeared to

be…springerlies, if Seth wasn't mistaken…onto the table
with the other baked goods that each member of the neurology unit had brought for today's party to celebrate their
co-worker's engagement.

Unfortunately, Prudence being Prudence, she put just a
little too much effort into the action, something that resulted in sending the container careering down the entire
length of the table. Not just that, but it ricocheted off every
other container in its way, and sent nearly half of them
tumbling over the edge of the table before falling and spill-
ing open itself.

Yep, springerlies for sure, Seth thought as they went skit-
tering across the floor. Broken springerlies now. Broken
springerlies with, he noted further, black, burned-to-a-crisp
bottoms.

What *had* her parents been thinking when they named
her Prudence?

She didn't even seem to notice what had happened, so
automatic were her gestures as she went to clean up the
mess. Then again, Seth thought, this was pretty much standard procedure for her, from what he'd witnessed in the
past, so it was really no surprise that she found this to be
no surprise.

"I'm sorry I'm so late," she said as she collected
crushed cookies from the floor, speaking, evidently, to both
nobody and everybody in the room. "Tanner was *so* into
the separation thing today. I didn't think I'd ever get away
from the day-care center."

Tanner, Seth knew, was Prudence's nine-month-old son,
whose acquaintance he had first made when the lad was all
of ten hours old. Although Seth worked in neurology, he
often spent his breaks and lunch hours in the hospital nursery, not just to cozy up to the neonatal nurses—who were
notoriously, in a word, hot—but also to cozy up to their
infant charges—who were notoriously, in a word, adorable.

To put it mildly, Seth had a real soft spot for kids. Someday he hoped to have one or two—or ten—of his own. And now, at the ripe old age of thirty-three, he was beginning to think seriously about the whole family thing. The problem was, biologically speaking, anyway, he himself didn't have all the necessary equipment for creating a family. In addition to a womb, he was going to need a second set of chromosomes for everything to work out the way it was supposed to work out. And so far he just hadn't met the right second set of chromosomes. Or the right womb, for that matter.

And lately he was beginning to think he never would.

For some reason that thought sent his gaze bouncing from the top half of Prudence's scrubs to the bottom half, which was currently sticking out from beneath the table as she reached for the last of the broken cookies. Yep. Nice curves indeed. Nice, round, lush, fertile curves, he couldn't help but notice. And he'd seen her with her son on a number of occasions. A more loving woman didn't exist anywhere in this universe.

Well, loving toward her son, at any rate, he amended. Where men were concerned, however, Prudence was considerably more…prudent. These days, at least. There had been a time, however, when… Well. Tanner was a pretty good indicator of Prudence's past where men were concerned. Still, she seemed to have learned her lesson there. Because she definitely kept her distance from the male half of the population these days. Much to Seth's unrelenting frustration.

"So the little tike was out of sorts today was he?" Seth asked as he approached her, knowing beforehand that she would respond to his query with a brittle smile.

Ah. Bingo. There it was now. As she backed herself out from under the table, she threw that smile over her shoulder at him, and *wham*. It hit its mark perfectly. Then there was another *wham*, but this time it was Prudence's head hitting the edge of the table as she tried to rise to standing.

"Ow," Seth said. "That had to hurt." Again, what *had* her parents been thinking?

Since the observation really required no comment, Prudence offered none. Instead, she finally pushed herself to standing and rubbed lightly at the crown of her head. But all she said was, "Yes. Tanner was out of sorts today. But it's not at all unusual for babies of nine months to go through separation anxiety like that," she added in the voice of experience.

"I don't doubt it for a moment," Seth concurred jovially. "It's not unusual for men of thirty-three, either." There. Let her make what she would of that.

What she made, he noted, was a funny little squinting type of face, an expression that made him smile. God, she was cute. And she really did have a nice neck. But she said nothing to demand clarification for his comment. Which was just as well, because he wasn't sure he wanted to clarify it—either to her, or to himself.

So instead he returned his attention to the heart-shaped cake on the table before him. Fine. He had the last scalpel available. It was nice to know he was wanted for *some*thing. Impulsively he decided that he would cut the cake—and idly ogle Prudence—stay long enough to consume a piece himself—and idly ogle Prudence—then he'd go home to lick his wounds—and idly fantasize about Prudence.

Carefully he bisected the confection from north to south and east to west, not worrying about whether the sizes were consistent. Everyone present in the break room was a medical professional, he reminded himself. Surely they could manage these small discrepancies without resorting to fist-icuffs.

After completing his task, Seth filled a plate with several of the homemade delicacies that constituted the celebratory buffet, then wasn't much surprised to find himself standing near—gosh, what do you know?—Prudence.

He always gravitated toward her, no matter where either of them happened to be. It was some kind of strange torture game he played with himself. He didn't for a moment understand his fascination with her, nor did he pursue it these days—not with any real enthusiasm. Not in any way that she would notice, at any rate. Nor in any way that anyone else would notice, either, for that matter.

At least, he hoped nobody else noticed. It would be so embarrassing to be thought of as pathetic. Even if pathetic was exactly the way he felt around Prudence Holloway. Even if pathetic was how he was beginning to think he was destined to be.

Though Seth *never* lacked for feminine companionship—well, never except today, he reminded himself morosely—the companionship with which he usually found himself generally left him reluctant to continue the relationship for very long. These days it seemed as though his temporary relationships were growing more and more temporary and he was feeling less and less satisfaction from them. Why that might be he couldn't possibly say. But there was no question that it was getting harder and harder to feel fulfilled in his personal life.

Not to be misconstrued, however—Seth did like women, very much. All women, in fact. And until he'd met Prudence, until he'd spent time with her—most of it indulging in good-natured sparring—he'd been perfectly content with the variety of his social life. But lately, for…oh, about the past two years…the variety he had once found so enjoyable was somehow beginning to lose its appeal.

Living his life day by day, and woman by woman, had all been well and good for a while—actually, it had been all *very* good—but there was a restlessness rising in Seth of late that he would just as soon quell. Mainly because he suspected that it was a restlessness born of the desire to settle down. And settling down wouldn't be a problem, except for the fact that he didn't think he could manage it. He was socially gregarious by nature, and he had the attention span of a rabid badger. He wasn't sure he'd be good in a family situation, in spite of his affinity for children. He just wasn't a one-woman man.

He reminded himself that he was only thirty-three, that he still had plenty of years left before he was so doddering that he wouldn't be able to bounce a baby on his knee. Then he remembered that at thirty-three most men were at least attached to someone special. Hell, even his best friend, Reed Atchison, whom Seth had *never* thought to see attached, had recently married. Now he and his wife, Mindy, were expecting the arrival of their first child any minute.

Without meaning to, Seth let his gaze wander over to Prudence once again. She really was lovely, he thought. And she was a warm, witty, gentle woman—with others, at any rate, in spite of her prickliness where he was concerned. He just wished he could understand why she wanted nothing to do with him. And then for some reason—probably because after the day he'd had he was spoiling for a fight—Seth decided to find out.

"So, Prudence," he began, heedless of the fact that he was interrupting her conversation with another nurse. "You're pulling second shift on a Friday. How did that happen? Won't it play havoc with your plans for a romantic evening?"

With obvious reluctance she turned to face him, her expression one of unmistakable, and perfectly expected, annoyance. "Not that it's any of your business," she began lightly, "but I don't have any plans for a romantic evening."

"How shocking," Seth remarked.

"Ramona needed the night off, and I was available," Prudence said with finality.

"You're never available for me," he pointed out, loving the way her mouth tightened into a disapproving little moue at his comment. Oh, she was *soooo* transparent. She wanted him. He was—almost—sure of it.

She narrowed her eyes at him. "There's a good reason for that," she said.

"But you've never seen fit to tell me what it is."

She shrugged, but there wasn't an ounce of carelessness in the gesture. "I figure you're a big boy, a smart guy. You have a college degree, and—"

"Three of them, actually," Seth supplied helpfully, holding up his left hand with that many fingers to punctuate the claim.

"—and I knew you could figure it out for yourself," she finished, ignoring his interjection.

He pressed his index finger against his cheek and, for a moment, feigned deep consideration. Then, after a moment, he told her, "Nope. Sorry. Can't figure it out. You'll just have to spell it out for me."

She smiled mildly at him, but there was no warmth in the gesture. Seth could tell, because the temperature in the room seemed to drop twenty degrees at least as she completed it. "Gosh, then I guess you're just not the big Mr. Know-It-All you thought you were, are you?"

Seth sniffed indignantly. "Hey, that's *Dr.* Know-It-All to you, Prudence," he countered.

"And that's *Ms. Holloway,* to *you,* Dr. Know-It-All."

He sidled up closer to her, mainly because he knew it bugged the hell out of her whenever he sidled in her presence. But for every step he took toward her, she took a step back. The nurse with whom she'd been conversing seemed to sense that her presence was no longer noticed, and slipped off nearly undetected. Seth braved another small step toward Prudence, and she, in turn, claimed another giant step in retreat. Doing so, however, rather impeded her progress, because it left her flat against the wall, just inches from a corner that effectively closed the trap.

Such an *im*prudent move on her part, Seth thought.

He smiled his most predatory smile, set down his plate of goodies and covered what little distance between them remained. Then he flattened one palm against the wall near her head and opened the other on the wall at his shoulder level. At last, he thought, he had fair Prudence where he wanted her.

Now if he could just get rid of the dozen other people present, maybe he could coax her around to his way of thinking. His way of thinking being, of course, that the two of them belonged together. Preferably close together. Preferably naked. Preferably horizontal. Though there was a lot to be said for vertical, too....

"You know," he murmured smoothly, bringing his face closer to hers—no easy feat, seeing as how she stood a good eight inches shorter than he. "A lot of the nurses here—a lot of the doctors, too—call me something other than Dr. Know-It-All."

"Do tell," she remarked dryly.

She almost convinced him that she was completely unmoved by his nearness, but Seth, ever vigilant, had noted the way the pulse at the base of her throat had quickened when he drew closer. Now he noted further that, currently, that pulse was pretty much dancing a samba. He also saw that her cheeks had warmed to pink, that her eyelids were lowering over darkly passionate eyes, and that her lips had parted in faint—but undeniable—desire.

Well, well, well, what have we here? he wondered. He hadn't had a chemistry lesson like this since he was an undergrad. Who knew?

He inhaled a slow, deep breath, then released it leisurely,

intentionally fanning the bare skin of her throat when he did. Again her pulse jumped, and her pupils dilated to nearly eclipse the pale green of her irises. Oh, she did have lovely eyes, he thought. Lovely, radiant, passionate eyes.

Eyes that held no secrets.

And for the first time in two years, Seth began to realize that Prudence wasn't *quite* as unaffected by him as she tried to let on. Now if he could just get her to admit that to herself....

"No, what they call me behind my back," he said softly, "is Dr....Irresistible. Of course, I myself," he hastily qualified, "much prefer Dr. Irrepressible, which, to my way of thinking, suits me much better. Dr. Irresistible is just a tad forward, don't you think? I would never presume to be irresistible. Even if," he couldn't quite stop himself from adding, "many women do find me just that."

Prudence expelled a sound that was decidedly unimpressed. But her pulse still jumped, and her eyes still grew dangerously dark. "Yeah, and some of them," she said, just a little shakily, Seth noticed, "me included, call you Dr.—"

Quickly, he moved one hand to her hair, skimming his palm deftly over the dark curls in an effort to unbalance her and to cut off whatever she had been about to say. And, he might as well just admit it, because it was something he'd been wanting to do for a long, long time.

"—Insufferable," she finished, anyway, jerking her head to the side in an effort to end his soft caress. "They—and I—call you Dr. Insufferable."

Well, this was news to Seth. No one, absolutely *no one*— no one of the feminine persuasion, at any rate—found him insufferable. Inspirational, impressive, incomparable, intrepid, sure. And of course, irresistible. And okay, maybe impertinent, impetuous, irreverent and incorrigible, on occasion. But insufferable? Him? No way. That was…inconceivable.

Seth shook his head—imperceptibly—and forced himself to turn the page in his mental thesaurus. Unfortunately, moving from the letter *I* just landed him with a bunch of *J* words—jerk, jester, juvenile, for example—which were no help at all. So he turned his attention back to the matter at hand.

"Prudence," he said, swallowing a chuckle, as always overcome by the inappropriateness of her name, "I think you're making that up."

The sound she expelled this time was even less impressed than the last one she'd made—but was still much too shaky for it to be nonchalant. "You have no idea," she told him.

He nodded. Of that, if nothing else, he was certain. Where Prudence Holloway was concerned, he never knew quite what to think. In spite of his conviction, however, he murmured, "Oh, really? Funny, but I actually have a few ideas where you're concerned."

"None of them decent, I'm sure," she said.

He smiled. "Well, of course not. Where would be the fun in that?"

"Dr. Mahoney," she began.

"Seth," he quickly corrected her. "How many times have I asked you to call me Seth?"

"Dr. Mahoney," she tried again, more forcefully this time. "If you'll excuse me, I'm due at the nurses' station."

Her voice was breathless and a couple of octaves lower than normal. Something about it made Seth's blood run hot—well, hotter than usual, anyway—and he couldn't quite bring himself to move out of her way, even though that was clearly what she was instructing him to do. He only continued to study her face and to lightly twine a dark curl around his index finger. And he realized then that the

color of her eyes reminded him of the shallow waters that
lapped at Caribbean beaches.

Someday, he thought, letting his mental meanderings
drift to fantasies again, maybe she'd accompany him on a
little trip down to that part of the world. They could charter
a sailboat, just the two of them, and sail indolently from
one tranquil harbor to another. They could make sweet love
beneath a blue sky and fiery sun, swim naked in cool waters, and then, when the moon hung high in the sky like a
bright silver dollar, make love again. Yeah, if only she'd—

"*Now.*"

That single word, uttered with such force and insistence,
snapped Seth right back to the present. Fine. She didn't
want to take a little sentimental journey right now. He could
handle that. He could. He had other things he had to do,
anyway. Like go home—alone—and eat dinner—alone—
and spend Friday night doing nothing—alone.

Damn, he hated being alone.

As he took a step backward—a very slow step backward—he realized he simply could not let Prudence go
without making one last effort to win her over.

"So you'll be getting off at eleven tonight, right?" he
asked smoothly. "Still time to enjoy a romantic evening
with someone you love."

She smiled seductively at his suggestion, then nodded
slowly, temptingly, as she unfolded her fingers over the
center of his chest. At her unexpected, not-so-subtle acqui-
escence, Seth's heart began to hammer hard in his chest,
his body heat shot up into triple figures, and his libido
hummed with anticipation. Wow. This was going to be easier than he thought.

"You know," she said in a low, throaty voice, "you're
right. I will have time to spend the evening with someone
I love. And I know just the guy I'd like to spend it with."

Seth's heart took flight at the look in her eyes. Finally

she was coming around. Finally she would admit what he'd known all along. Finally she was going to accept the fact that the two of them were meant for each other. At least for one delirious evening.

"Do you now?" he asked.

She nodded that slow, seductive nod again, smiled that tempting little smile. "Oh, yeah. He's gorgeous, smart, fun to be around…"

"Yes?" Seth prodded.

"He's someone I'm looking forward to spending, not just the evening, but the entire night with."

"Do tell."

"And not just tonight, either, but *every* night."

"Yes?"

"For a long, *long* time."

"Oh, Prudence," Seth murmured low, for her ears only. "It's about time you accepted the unavoidable fact of what's happening between us."

He was reaching up to cover her hand with his when her charming smile turned menacing. Before he realized what was happening, she flattened her palm fiercely and shoved him backward. Hard. He righted himself just before toppling backward onto his…his…pride, but could do nothing about the heat of embarrassment that flamed inside him as he watched her move easily away.

"My son," she tossed over her shoulder as she went. "I plan to spend this evening, and every other evening I have available, with Tanner." And with that, she spun around and left the break room, without a backward glance.

You idiot, Seth chastised himself as he watched her go. When would he learn? Prudence Holloway had never, did never, would never, want him. Why couldn't he just leave it alone? Why did he keep going back for more, when it was abundantly clear that his efforts were pointless?

Because he just couldn't stay away, he answered himself

immediately. That was why. She was Nurse Irresistible. And besides, there was a hint of something…something indefinable…in her eyes whenever she looked at him. He couldn't quite say for sure what it was, but it was there whenever he drew close enough to see it. And it was that something indefinable that held Seth in thrall. Until he could find out exactly what it was that bound the two of them—because there was most definitely *something* binding them—he couldn't let it go.

He told himself that it was the heat of two dozen eyes on his back—and *not* because Prudence had shoved him aside—that made him lose his appetite. He spun around as quickly as she had, only to find everyone else in the room dropping their gazes hastily to their plates. Sheepishly he tugged his necktie to straighten it, then rolled his shoulders as if totally unconcerned.

Then, to the room at large, he said, "She wants me. You know she wants me. It's obvious. I'm—almost—sure of it."

As he had known it would, a ripple of laughter lightened the mood, and Seth punctuated it with a dashing smile of his own. It was widely known at Seton General that he and Prudence indulged in such antics frequently. Everyone knew it was all in fun. Everyone knew it was all in jest. Everyone knew that Seth wasn't really as crazy about Prudence as he let on. And everyone knew that Prudence was being a good sport about it all.

Everyone knew that.

Everyone except Seth. And maybe, just maybe, Prudence. He only wished he knew what to do about clarifying it all for the two of them. And he only wished he could put whatever it was burning between them to rest, once and for all.

Two

Even after detouring through the women's room on her way, by the time Pru sat down at the nurses' station in neurology, she still hadn't quite recovered from her little...whatever it had been...with Dr. Mahoney. Her heart was still hammering hard in her chest, her blood was still fizzing at light speed through her veins, the strings of her heart were still zinging to beat the band, and her brain was a muddled mass of confusion and—dammit—desire.

Worse than all that, however, her stomach was grumbling hungrily in protest of the fact that it had been anticipating a plate full of cookies by now. *Hey, too bad,* Pru told her noisy belly. There was nothing to be done for it. No way would she go back to that break room as long as Seth Mahoney was still in the building. Or still in the state of New Jersey, for that matter.

Boy, she'd really been looking forward to scarfing up a few of those springerlies, too, broken, burned bottoms and all. She'd had to miss lunch today, because Tanner had been clingy and fretful, and she just hadn't had it in her to disregard his demands.

He was such a great kid, after all, and normally made surprisingly few demands on her. Usually he was a pretty free-wheeling, independent little guy, which had made his moodiness today all the more distressing. And since he'd been so unwilling to part with Pru at the hospital's day care center, she'd used up what little time she had left before her shift to play with him and read to him, in the hope that it would make his transition a little easier.

Ultimately that plan had worked out nicely. By the time she'd left him in the care of her good buddy, Teresa, the little guy was cooing and laughing and having a great time. But then *Pru* had been cranky and out of sorts, thanks to being so hungry. She'd planned on eating enough cookies to tide her over until her 6:30 dinner break. But she wasn't about to return to the neurology department's engagement party for Renee, with Dr. Mahoney on the make.

Then again, she thought dryly, when was Seth Mahoney *not* on the make? He was the biggest lurer of women to come along since a snake unwound itself from around an apple tree. And she did *not* want to find herself the object of his temptation. Again. It had been hard enough to resist him the first time he'd tried tempting her—which had been about thirty seconds after starting his first shift at Seton General two years ago. The second time he had tried tempting her had been even more difficult—and had been about forty-five seconds after starting his first shift at Seton General two years ago. Not to mention the third time—sixty seconds after starting his first shift. And the fourth time, at two minutes. And the…

Well, it just never got any easier, that was all. And just how dumb did that make her, wanting to succumb to a man like him, even if she had been successful—so far—in keeping her distance? Seth Mahoney was the very last kind of man Pru needed in her life. He was incorrigible. Immature. Impulsive. Even if he *was* Dr. Irresistible.

Which, fine, she conceded, was a suitable enough nickname for him, because he was sort of…you know… irresistible. But that was only because he was charming and cute and, okay, a little adorable, too, in a blond, blue-eyed, all-American-boy kind of way. And, okay, so maybe there were times—not that many, though—when Pru caught herself ogling him as he strode down a hallway or when she ran into him in the cafeteria or some such thing.

And yeah, yeah, sure, okay, he showed up in her dreams on occasion, in a fashion that was anything but professional—mainly because he was undressed and the two of them were…well, never mind. And all right, yes, truth be told, she'd even fantasized about him once or twice when she was fully conscious and he was fully clothed.

But honestly. A more philandering, womanizing playboy she had never met. Ever since his arrival at Seton General, Seth Mahoney had left a string of broken hearts, of both the RN and MD variety, in his glorious, blond, blue-eyed wake. He was everything she *didn't* want or need in a man. Succumbing to him would be…would be…

Well, it would be totally irresponsible.

And *irresponsible* was the one thing that Pru Holloway totally, absolutely, definitely, unequivocally, at all costs, avoided being. These days, at least. No way would she tolerate being called irresponsible. So no way was she going to take up with Seth Mahoney.

He was in no way husband-and-father material, and these days that was exactly what Pru wanted and needed—and deserved—in a man. Someone who was upright, forthright, do right. Someone who wanted to build a family, not abandon one. Seth Mahoney had way too much in common with

Tanner's father, she recalled, not for the first time. Both were golden-haired, ocean-eyed charmers. Both had a way of making a woman—any woman—feel as if she were their one-and-only, forever-after kind of love. Both were totally irresistible.

And both had the emotional maturity of thirteen-year-olds.

A year and a half ago, the day Pru had realized she was pregnant, she had hesitated before telling her boyfriend, Kevin, the news. She'd been stunned at first by the knowledge of her impending motherhood—the two of them *had* been using birth control but had become part of that slight percentage of failure. Yet after giving her condition some serious thought, Pru had been surprised to discover, even then, that she wasn't all that upset to find herself pregnant.

In the long run—once the shock had worn off, anyway—she'd come to understand that it wasn't the idea of impending motherhood that had really bothered her then. No, what had really bothered her had been the idea of marrying Kevin. As much as she'd told herself she loved the guy, Pru just hadn't been able to quite visualize living with him…day after day after day…week after week after week…month after month after month…for the rest of her natural life. Deep down she'd known, even then, that he wasn't a forever-after kind of guy.

But she had wanted to behave responsibly, and that meant telling Kevin he would be a father and then marrying Kevin so that their baby would benefit from the presence of two loving parents. Unfortunately, she discovered right away that there were a couple of unforeseen factors she hadn't fully considered where their relationship was concerned. One of those factors was that Kevin was a complete jerk. The other factor was that said jerk took off for Jerkland the day after Pru broke the news to him, and he was never heard from again.

They had made a date to meet for dinner, to talk about their situation once Kevin had had twenty-four hours to get used to the idea of his impending fatherhood. But Kevin had evidently decided what he wanted to do in about twenty-four seconds. Because he never showed up at the restaurant. And when Pru went to his apartment, she discovered that it had been cleaned out. Completely. When she went to the Chevron station where he worked, she was told he had quit his job that morning and had left no forwarding address where he could be contacted. According to his boss, he'd cited "family problems" as the reason for his abrupt departure.

Yeah, right. *Family problems,* Pru repeated to herself now. His *problem* was that he hadn't wanted a *family.*

She sighed with heartfelt frustration, pushed the sad memories away and sat down in her chair at the nurses' station. She knew she was better off this way, that any life she might have tried to build with Kevin would have come tumbling down around her feet in no time flat. Better that she had discovered what kind of man he was before Tanner's birth, than to risk having Tanner grow attached to his father and suffer the grief of his loss.

A baby needed to be loved and wanted. Kevin had obviously felt neither emotion for his son, and Tanner would have eventually figured that out. But Pru had enough love and want in her heart for two people and then some, and she gave it all to her child. Someday, she was confident, she would meet a man with whom she could share those feelings, too, a man who would be both perfect husband and perfect father material. For now, however, she was truly content to be alone.

Well, pretty content to be alone, at any rate. Kind of content. In a way. Being alone was certainly better than being with someone who didn't love her. Of that much she was absolutely sure.

"Why, Prudence Holloway, as I live and breathe!"

Pru's head snapped up at the summons, and her gaze fell on a woman who appeared to have exited from one of the patient rooms that surrounded the nurses' station. She studied the woman intently in silence for a moment, and although she looked a bit familiar, Pru couldn't quite place where she might have met her.

"Yes?" she said, not quite able to hide her confusion. "I'm Pru Holloway. Can I help you?"

The woman drew nearer and frowned at her, but the gesture seemed playful somehow. She wore a pale-lavender dress that shimmered beneath the fluorescent lighting overhead in a way that only pure silk can. Elegant pearls circled her neck and were fastened in her ears, and a good half dozen rings—all quite sparkly in a rainbow of hues—decorated the fingers of both hands. Her cosmetics were artfully applied, her strawberry-blond hair swept back from her face by an expert hand.

In no way was she the kind of woman who traveled in Pru's social circle. This woman was obviously wealthy and refined, and used to the finer things in life.

"Don't tell me you don't remember me," she said. "Easton High School? Class of '90?"

Pru studied the woman harder. If this woman was, as she seemed to be claiming, a member of Pru's senior class, then Pru should *definitely* remember her. No way would she forget anyone at Easton High in her native Pittsburgh, in spite of there having been 240 members of her graduating class, and in spite of the fact that she had gone out of her way to avoid every last one of them for the past ten years.

No way would she forget the people who had dubbed her, in the year book's senior class superlatives, "Most Irresponsible."

The dubious distinction had only crowned what had been four years of taunting from her classmates, and it had brought with it many chuckles throughout her senior year. Pru, however, had never been the one laughing. No, that particular pleasure had fallen to all her classmates, who had delighted in replaying, time and time again, all the instances when she had behaved a bit...oh...irresponsibly.

Pru herself had never understood the humor everyone else had found in having awarded her such a label. Even if she *had* been a tad, oh...irresponsible...over the years, that was no reason for her high school class to have voted her such.

And then to have printed the distinction in the senior yearbook.

Beside a photograph of her dangling upside down over the side of a cliff, with a rappelling line wrapped around her ankle after she had...irresponsibly...tried to climb it without the benefit of lessons.

And above a list of other activities—at least a dozen of them—that had been a trifle, oh...irresponsible.

For everyone to see. For everyone to laugh about. For all eternity.

It really wasn't so much that Pru had been irresponsible, she tried to reassure herself now, as she had for so many years. No, it had just been that she just didn't like to be bothered with taking the extra time out to learn to do things or read the instructions or follow rules.

These days, of course, she was nothing like she had been in high school. Nothing at all. No way. Motherhood had brought with it an enormous amount of responsibility. And Pru was proud of herself for having risen to the occasion so nicely. She took good care of her son, provided a life for him that was, if not luxurious, certainly more than adequate. And these days, those rash impulses that had been the bane of her youth were nowhere to be found.

At least, she was pretty sure they were nowhere to be found. It had been quite some time since she'd behaved rashly or impulsively. And she tried very hard to keep it that way. Of course, one could argue that her incessant preoccupation with one Seth Mahoney might be construed as slightly, oh…irresponsible. But she hadn't acted on that preoccupation, had she? She hadn't done anything there that might lead to behavior that was, oh…irresponsible. She hadn't been at all impulsive or spontaneous or impetuous or even irresponsible.

Well, not yet, anyway, a little voice at the back of her head taunted her.

Ignoring the voice, Pru turned her attention back to the woman who had summoned her, resolved to decipher her identity.

As if sensing Pru's determination, the woman smiled and said, "Oh, all right, I admit it. I've changed a bit." She touched a finger to a delicate curl dancing over her forehead. "I used to be a dishwater blonde," she confessed. "And I've lost about twenty-five pounds since we sat next to each other in Mrs. Clement's literary social criticism class."

Pru gaped, then covered her mouth. "Hazel Dubrowski?" she said.

The other woman's smile turned radiant. "In person."

"Oh, my gosh," Pru cried, stunned by the transformation. "You look incredible."

"Yes, I know," Hazel agreed without a trace of modesty.

Now that Pru knew the woman's identity, she could definitely see signs of seventeen-year-old Hazel Dubrowski lurking there. Still, ten years—and heaven knew how many trips to the salon—had given her old schoolmate a totally new appearance.

"It's actually Hazel Debbit now," she told Pru as she strode forward, pausing at the counter of the nurses' station to drum perfectly manicured, plum-colored fingernails over the Formica covering. "I got married three years ago. My

husband is the CEO of a Fortune 500 company that his
father founded.''

''Is that what you're doing here in South Jersey?'' Pru
asked. ''Do you and your husband live here?''

Hazel shook her head. ''No, we live in Pittsburgh, but
my in-laws are here.'' She jutted a thumb over her shoulder,
toward the room she had exited a moment ago. ''My father-
in-law was in having some tests done. Nothing major,'' she
hastened to add. ''He's fine. In fact, my husband is helping
him pack up his things now, because he's just been released.''

''Well, that's good news.''

The other woman nodded. ''And now I run into you after
all this time. Prudence Holloway. I can't believe it. Small
world. So what have you been doing since graduation? Nobody's heard from you since you left Pittsburgh, especially
now that your folks moved.''

Yes, well, there was a good reason for that, Pru recalled.
Namely that she didn't want to speak to anyone in Pittsburgh, especially now that her folks had moved. But she
didn't think it would be a good idea to tell Hazel that.

''I've been living here in South Jersey for about six years
now, ever since getting my nursing degree. I needed a
change,'' she said casually by way of an explanation. At
least, she hoped she'd sounded casual. Because it really
hadn't been so much because she needed a change that had
made her leave Pittsburgh. It had been more because she
had needed an entirely new life.

''Wow,'' Hazel said, obviously surprised by this news.
''You got a nursing degree?'' She shook her head in disbelief. ''When I saw you standing out here, I figured you
must be a hospital volunteer or something. I had no idea
you were actually a *nurse*. I mean, that takes drive and
ambition. You really have to dedicate yourself. I can't be-

lieve you lasted through four years of college and nurse's training. That's amazing.''

Yeah, Pru thought morosely, and now that Hazel did know she was a nurse, she'd probably be wondering if her father-in-law had been safe while assigned to this unit. Because, hey, to everyone at Easton High, Prudence Holloway would live forever as ''Most Irresponsible,'' dangling upside down from a rappelling line.

''I mean,'' Hazel added, as if she really, really, *really* wanted to drive home her point, ''I can't imagine *anyone* giving *you* a degree in something like *nursing*. It just sort of defies logic.''

Pru drew herself up with all the dignity she could muster. She was remembering Hazel pretty well now and recalling that, by their senior year, she had been like everyone else at Easton. Always looking for a new way to tear Pru down. Always poking fun. Always laughing.

''Yeah, well, even more astonishing,'' Pru couldn't help adding, ''I graduated from nursing school at the top of my class.''

This time Hazel was the one to gape. ''Get out,'' she said. ''Where did you go? Did you take one of those International School of Bartending nursing courses?''

Somehow, Pru managed to keep her growl of discontent to herself. ''No. I went to Penn State,'' she said.

Hazel only shook her head slowly as she studied Pru. ''Boy, you just never know with some schools, do you?''

What Pru knew was that there was no reason to continue with this conversation. Just as everything—and everyone—else in high school had, it would only serve to demoralize her further. She'd come a long way in the ten years that had passed since graduation, and she wasn't about to go back. Hazel Dubrowski Debbit just served as a reminder of how good Pru had it these days, having left all that behind.

''Well,'' she said coolly to Hazel as she picked up a file

from the counter that she really didn't need at the moment. "It was good seeing you again, Hazel. Give my regards to everybody in Pittsburgh."

She hoped she'd made clear her subtle but suitable hint that their conversation—and all other contact—was concluded, but Hazel obviously didn't take it. Because even when Pru glanced down as if looking for something else, her old classmate closed what little distance remained between her and the station, then folded her arms over the counter. When Pru glanced up, arching her eyebrows in silent query, Hazel only smiled.

"You'll be at the reunion next month, right?"

Although Pru had received her invitation—wondering, frankly, how and why the reunion committee had tracked her down—she had ignored it. No way would she subject herself to something like a ten-year reunion. Hey, she was happy these days. Why mess with a good thing? Especially since, considering her present situation of single motherhood, she would only be laughed at all over again?

Because what could possibly be more irresponsible than being knocked up and abandoned, right? The last thing Pru needed was for her senior class to be hearing about *that*. "No, I hadn't planned to attend," she said. Then, unable to quite quell the ten-year-old hurt that had haunted her, she found herself adding, "Do you honestly think I want to go to a ten-year reunion and see a bunch of people who voted me 'most irresponsible' in the senior class superlatives? Why should I put myself through that? High school was bad enough the first time around. Who needs to go through it a second time?"

Hazel chuckled. "Oh, come on, Pru," she said. "Lighten up. It'll be fun. Aren't you curious to see how everyone turned out?"

"No," she answered honestly.

The other woman's smile turned positively predatory.

Oh, yeah. Now she remembered Hazel Dubrowski. Really well. She'd been one of the most carnivorous members of the senior class. In fact, now that Pru thought more about it, she recalled that Hazel had been on the yearbook staff and had been the one who spearheaded the senior superlatives in the first place. And the one who spearheaded the campaign was the one who usually wound up deciding the winners, based on the prevailing winds.

Sure, Pru could see how she might have been viewed as irresponsible back then. But Hazel was the one who would have created the category. And somehow, Pru was certain she'd done it on purpose, just so she could hang the crown of thorns on Pru's head. And that was because, Pru also remembered now, Jimmy Abersold had asked *her* to the junior prom, instead of Hazel.

Oh, it was all coming back to her now. Funny, how selective a person's memory could be about something like high school—until that memory was forcibly jarred by some baaaad karma, like Hazel was bringing with her now.

"Well, I'm sure they're all anxious to see how *you* turned out," she told Pru with a smile that was at first knowing and then suspicious. "And just how *did* you turn out, anyway?" she asked further. "I mean, it's one thing to be a nurse, but what else is going on with you, Pru? I kind of always figured you for the type to wind up knocked up and abandoned somewhere."

Pru felt a cool weight settle in the pit of her stomach at hearing her own words—her own fears—echoed back at her. But even if she had indeed ended up exactly the way Hazel had known she would, Pru refused to capitulate to the other woman's meanness.

Schooling her features into the blandest expression she could, she replied evenly, "Really."

Hazel nodded. "Oh, yeah. I imagine most of the class of '90 assumed the same thing. Even if you were Little

Miss Goody-Two-Shoes for the most part, someone as irresponsible as you were was bound to wind up pregnant and alone and relying on welfare. It's just the logical conclusion to make.''

Amazed at her ability to remain civil, Pru repeated, ''Really.''

And in that moment she knew she had made the right decision in disregarding the invitation to her ten-year reunion. There was no way she would let her senior class discover firsthand just how right they'd been about her all along. The last thing she needed was for 240 people to laugh and point and say, ''Man, it's even worse than we thought it would be. She really did get knocked up and abandoned.'' And worse, ''Hey, Pru, we told you so.'' And worse still, ''We knew what kind of person you were all along, even if you never believed it yourself.''

Hazel nodded again, more adamantly this time. ''But, gosh,'' she said, ''just look at you, all professional in your nurse's uniform. Maybe you *have* built a solid, responsible life for yourself. I suppose stranger things have happened. Probably. Maybe. In outer space somewhere.''

A solid, responsible life, Pru repeated to herself, ignoring the sarcasm inherent in the response. She hoped the heat she felt flaming in her midsection didn't show up in her face.

''I mean,'' Hazel went on, as if she sensed Pru's discomfort and wanted very much to compound it, ''for all I know, you're happily married, and you and your husband have a big, beautiful house right here in Cherry Hill. Hey, for all I know, you married a *doctor*.'' Hazel's smile, however, indicated what a joke she thought that was. ''I can just see you subscribing to the orchestra, the ballet, and the theater,'' she went on blithely, clearly not meaning a word of what she said. ''You probably spend your spare time volunteering at an art museum or being active in your garden club and your reading group and your cooking club. And your kids are probably all beautiful and smart and going to private school. Tell me I'm right,'' Hazel dared her. ''Tell me that's exactly the way you live these days.''

Pru swallowed hard, wishing she could agree with every word that Hazel said. Not because she wanted it to be true, and not because she particularly aspired to such a grand life. But because she knew that once her old classmate found out the truth, Hazel would gleefully recount the situation to every single member of the Easton class of '90 when she went to the reunion.

Oh, I saw Pru Holloway last month, and she hasn't changed at all. She's still totally irresponsible. Got herself knocked up by some jerk who dumped her. Now she's a single mother struggling to pay the bills on some dinky apartment. She's probably on food stamps and has credit-card debt out the wazoo. Most likely her kid'll end up in jail. Then we honest taxpayers will have to pay both *their ways through life.*

Oh, yeah. She could see it now. Everyone in the Easton High class of '90 ought to have a lot of laughs at her expense. And even if Pru wasn't planning to attend herself, she didn't want her title of ''Most Irresponsible'' to be perpetuated forever. She hated to be the butt of jokes, even in absentia.

But the fact was, she forced herself to admit, that the label still fit. As much as she had tried to change her ways, and as much as she hated to admit it, she *was* irresponsible. She always had been. She always would be. She didn't know why she tried to kid herself otherwise.

There was no husband, no house, no lifestyle of forthright responsibility. There were no subscriptions to the arts—hey, who could afford it? There was no volunteer work—hey, who had time? There were no garden clubs, reading groups or cooking clubs. The closest thing Pru had to a garden was the questionably breathing African Violet on her kitchen windowsill, the one she—irresponsibly—kept forgetting to water. The only books she'd bought in the last year had been about infant care and breastfeeding, and even those she'd only—irresponsibly—skimmed. As for cooking, well…she wondered if microwaving pot pies and Beefaroni on a regular basis counted for anything. Anything other than being totally irresponsible about one's health.

And then, of course, there was that business about having been knocked up and abandoned, Pru reminded herself unnecessarily. Yep, pretty much the ultimate in irresponsible behavior.

"So just what *is* your life like these days, Pru?" Hazel challenged her again, smiling in a way that indicated she just couldn't *wait* to hear. Mainly because she just couldn't *wait* to tell everyone they knew that Prudence Holloway had turned out exactly the way they had all known she would.

Resigned to her fate, Pru opened her mouth to confess.

But she was intercepted by a deep baritone that answered for her, "Her life is pretty much exactly the way you described it."

She spun around to find Seth Mahoney standing behind her, smiling that incredibly charming smile that made every female in a fifty-foot radius melt in a puddle of ruined womanhood at his feet. Hazel Dubrowski Debbit, Pru realized upon turning her attention back to her old classmate, was no exception. Because she stood gaping at Dr. Mahoney as if he were a great, big, hot-fudge sundae with marshmallows and strawberries on top.

"Who're you?" Hazel asked, heedless of the lack of courtesy in the command.

He extended his hand toward her and jacked up the power on his smile about a hundred kilowatts. Pru was nearly blinded. And her heart went *vah-rooooom.* "I'm Seth Mahoney," he said smoothly, easily, sexily, taking Hazel's hand in his. "I'm Prudence's husband."

Three

My what?

For a moment, Pru feared she had spoken the question aloud—loudly aloud—then realized the echo she was hearing was only in her brain.

Oh, no, she thought, when she understood what Dr. Mahoney was doing. *Oh, no, please. Not that. Anything but that.* But before she could say a word to contradict him, he launched into what she was sure would become the biggest, fattest, whoppingest lie she had ever heard in her life.

"It's uncanny, really," he told Hazel, "how you hit on things so exactly." He dropped an arm casually around Pru's shoulder and pulled her close, and the vrooming in her heart compounded. "We do, in fact, have a big, beautiful house right here in Cherry Hill. Four thousand square feet, if you must know. And frankly, Hazel," he added, dropping his voice to a conspiratorial murmur, "you do seem like the type who must know."

He straightened again before continuing, then went on without care, "Pru, God love her, is active in so many things. In addition to her work here at the hospital, she is involved in nearly every one of those activities you listed. Just between you and me, I don't know how she does it. She's an amazing woman.

"Oh, and this," he added, picking up a framed photo of Tanner she kept at the nurse's station, "this is our son, Tanner." He thrust the picture at Hazel, who, still gaping, took it from him and dropped her gaze toward it. "He's nine months old. A great-looking kid and smart as a whip. He's the only one we have right now, but we're planning on at least two more. It goes without saying that they'll all be going to the finest school we can find for them." He turned to Prudence, beaming. "Right, honey?" he said.

Too stunned to do anything else, Pru nodded and replied faintly, "Right."

And then, catching her totally off guard, he bent his head and brushed his lips lightly, affectionately, over hers.

It was a brief, simple, chaste kiss. There was no reason for it to set off explosions throughout her midsection. There was no reason for it to send a sizzle of heat right through her body, from fingertips to toes. There was no reason why she should want to push herself up on tiptoe, wrap her arms around his neck, and pull him back down for a more thorough embrace, for a more demanding grope.

But that was exactly what she wanted to do. Those were exactly her responses. Even the merest touch of his mouth on hers had her brain scrambled and her libido in an uproar.

Dr. Mahoney, however, upon pulling back, looked as if what he'd just done was something he did every day. He gazed at her as if the two of them had been married for years. As if the two of them were irrevocably in love. As if the two of them were building a life together. As if the two of them had made a baby together.

Oh, no. Oh, no, please. Not that. Anything but that.

"I'm sorry," he said, turning back to Hazel. "What was your name again? I seem to have stumbled into this conversation somewhere in the middle. I missed the beginning part. I gather you're a friend of Prudence's from high school?"

Hazel nodded dumbly, numbly, as if she were still held in thrall by the golden, shining promise that was Seth Mahoney.

"Well, how nice," he said. "It's always good to run into an old friend and relive those glory days." He returned his attention to Pru, his back fully on Hazel now. And Pru could see by his expression that he knew exactly what Hazel had been pulling a moment ago, and it was his intention to bail Pru out. "Isn't it, sweetheart?" he added. "Isn't it *fun* to see people from high school that you honestly thought you would never, ever, see again for the rest of your natural life? Don't you just *love* that?"

His smile was absolutely devilish, and Pru couldn't help but succumb to it, to him. Trying not to giggle, she smiled back. "Oh, yeah," she agreed. "It's something, all right. Honey," she added belatedly, hoping she wasn't slathering it on too thick.

His expression told her that she probably was, but that he didn't have a problem with it. And then, as if to illustrate that very thing, he bent and kissed her quickly again. Simply, briefly, chastely. Explosively, hotly, uproariously. Part of her really wished he would stop doing that. But another—perhaps even larger—part of her, wished he would never, ever stop.

"So I guess this means you'll be coming to the reunion with Prudence, then, won't you?"

As one, Pru and Dr. Mahoney turned to Hazel. But he was the one to ask, "What do you mean? What reunion?"

Hazel uttered a soft sound of surprise. "Didn't she tell

you? Her ten-year high school reunion is next month. The invitations went out in January.''

"I…I didn't mention it…dear," Pru quickly replied, "because I know how, uh…how busy March is going to be, and I…I just didn't think I…that is, I didn't think *we*…would be able to make it."

Oh, well done, Pru, she said, congratulating herself. *My, but that had sounded convincing.*

"Oh, pooh," Hazel said with a dismissive wave of her hand. "It's been ten years. You could clear one weekend for the reunion. Besides," she hurriedly went on when Pru opened her mouth to object again, "considering the way you live now, you'd be crazy not to come to the reunion. Don't you want to rub everybody's nose in it about the 'Most Irresponsible' thing?"

"'The Most Irresponsible thing'?" Dr. Mahoney echoed, his interest quite clearly piqued on that score. His blue eyes fairly sparkled with mischief. "What's 'the Most Irresponsible thing'?"

Pru opened her mouth to respond, but this time it was Hazel who cut her off.

"You may not know this about your wife," she said to Dr. Mahoney, "but she hasn't always been the forthright, upstanding woman you made of her."

The blue eyes began to twinkle, Pru noticed. *Twinkle.* Of all things.

"Do tell," he said mildly.

Of course Hazel was perfectly willing to do just that. "Oh, you can't imagine some of the tight spots she found herself in when we were in high school."

"Tight?" he repeated. "Really? Such as…?"

Once more Hazel shot that careless hand forward. "Oh, heavens. Where to begin."

"Don't you have to make your rounds…sweetheart?" Pru asked impulsively, nudging the good doctor's arm from her shoulder with a single, careless shrug. "Surely you have patients waiting for you."

"Oh, they don't mind waiting a few minutes more," he assured her. "Now then, Hazel, you were saying…? About tight…spots?"

She dimpled prettily as she grinned at him. "Oh, it would take more than a few minutes to tell you all about Pru's misadventures," she said. "But to make a long story short, your wife was voted Most Irresponsible by the senior class of Easton High School ten years ago."

He gaped, feigning astonishment. At least, Pru could tell it was feigned. Hazel, however, seemed to be falling for it hook, line and sinker. "*My* Prudence?" he asked, splaying a hand open over his heart in disbelief. "*Irresponsible?* I don't believe it for a moment. I've never met a woman with her act more together than hers is."

Somehow, Pru managed to swallow the burst of hysterical laughter that wanted to leap out of her throat.

"She's amazing, the way she's organized our lives," he said further. Then, turning to ooze his charm all over Pru, he added, "I don't know what I'd do without her."

Something about the way he said that, and something about the glint of undisguised hunger in his eyes, made that vrooming in her chest start up again, and this time it didn't settle into idle. This time it just kept vrooming, as if very much in need of a new muffler. And Pru got hot all over again wondering just what, exactly, *muffling* would involve when it came to Seth Mahoney.

"Well, then," Hazel said, as if everything were settled. "What could be more responsible than the life you're leading these days, Pru? Now you *have* to be at the reunion. Come show everybody up. Let them see how wrong they were about you. Come say 'I told you so' to everyone."

Unable to come up with a good excuse not to, Pru turned to her newly acquired husband, silently demanding a reply from him. He had, after all, gotten her into this. The least he could do was dig her out again. But instead of offering her an adequate excuse, or even backing up the lame one that she had supplied about being too busy, Dr. Mahoney smiled a dangerously cryptic smile.

"Well, why the hell not?" he asked.

"What?" she exclaimed.

"Come on, Prudence, it'll be fun."

"But...but...but..." she said. Unfortunately her brain refused to budge from that one, not particularly polite, word.

"Oh, good," Hazel said, clearly delighted to have something to liven up the reunion.

Okay, this had gone far enough, Pru thought. No more fun and games, no matter how much Seth Mahoney seemed to be enjoying his little diversion. "Now wait a just minute," she began.

But once more Hazel cut her off. "I won't accept no for an answer."

"But—"

Hazel ignored the interjection and turned to Dr. Mahoney, obviously unable to resist him. "You'll make sure you change her mind about coming to the reunion next month."

"Of course," he said with utter confidence.

"But, Hazel—" Pru tried again.

"Good," she interrupted again. "I'll call Diane Magill tonight—oh, she was Diane Sorensen in high school," she added parenthetically to Pru before turning her attention back to Dr. Mahoney.

"But, Hazel, I—" Pru tried again.

"She's the reunion coordinator, and I'll tell her to put Prudence Holloway Mahoney and her luscious...uh...I mean, *lovely,* husband, Seth, down as yesses."

"But, Hazel, I don't—"

"I'll see you both—and that adorable little baby of

yours—there.'' She smiled brightly again, more at Dr. Mahoney than at Pru, Pru noted.

"But, Hazel, I don't think—''

Unfortunately, Pru was forced to accept the fact that Hazel had stopped listening to her a long time ago. Like maybe ten years ago. Because with that final parting shot, Hazel Dubrowski Debbit, who had once thoroughly upended Pru's life, spun on her heel and walked away, having thoroughly upended Pru's life once again.

Oh, no, she thought. *Oh, no, please. Not that. Anything but that...*

Seth watched Witch Hazel saunter saucily down the corridor, and he marveled that human beings could behave so abominably. Not that he was surprised by the woman's reaction to Prudence. Au contraire. Unfortunately, he knew better than many what kind of cruelty people were capable of feeling and displaying. In spite of that, however, he still held fast to the conviction that, deep down, the average person was essentially good. Decent. Loving. Kind.

Go figure.

He braved neither a word nor a look toward the nurse who stood silent at his side. He wasn't sure yet whether or not Prudence would slap him silly for meddling in the circumstances that had erupted between her and her former classmate. He only knew that when he'd passed by the nurse's station on his way out, and had heard her being bullied by the obnoxious, pretentious Hazel, he had reacted instinctively. The situation between the two women had been clear, but knowing Prudence—and Seth did know Prudence, though not nearly as well as he would like—she would have taken the high road in the matter, and let her old high school chum run roughshod over her in the process.

And Seth just couldn't let that happen. Prudence was a

nice person, and she deserved better than to be belittled by some smug poseur. Besides, he had no qualms about taking the low road himself, having used it as a shortcut through life on many occasions. He didn't suffer fools lightly, nor did he tolerate meanness. And Prudence being Prudence, well…

He just hadn't wanted to see her get hurt, that was all.

Once Witch Hazel was completely out of sight, he sensed more than saw her turn her entire body to face him. Even at that, however, he couldn't quite bring himself to look at her. Mainly because he didn't trust himself not to react when he did. And he feared that his reaction would be to pull her into his arms and kiss her senseless. That was, after all, his reaction to Prudence Holloway no matter what she was doing. And those two brief, innocent kisses during their little show for Hazel had only inflamed Seth's desire to steal a few—less brief, less innocent—more.

"Why did you do that?" she asked him softly. There was no venom, no accusation in her voice when she uttered the question, only simple curiosity.

"Why did I do what?" he asked mildly, pretending to have no knowledge of what had just happened. He did turn then, tipping his head a bit to study her face as he asked the question. She stood more than a half foot shorter than he, but somehow she'd never seemed in any way small to him.

"Why did you lie for me?" she asked pointedly. "Why did you come to my rescue that way? You didn't have a stake in this thing at all. And after the way I've treated you…" She swallowed hard, her green eyes dark and earnest, then tried again. "After the way I've treated you, I wouldn't blame you if you just left me twisting in the wind. I probably deserved it."

He shook his head. "You didn't deserve to be left hanging, Prudence. And you certainly didn't deserve the kind of attack that Witch Hazel was loosing on you."

She smiled at the moniker. "You know, I used to think of her that way, too, when I was in high school. She was never very nice."

Seth nodded. "Unfortunately, a lot of that goes around in high school."

Prudence nodded in return, clearly understanding. "You still haven't told me why you bailed me out in my time of need."

He hesitated before answering, reluctant to divulge his reason. He started to lift a hand, as if by doing so he might pull the right words from thin air, then hastily changed his mind and moved it toward Prudence's hair instead. But the moment he began to twist an errant curl around his finger, the moment he saw her eyes widen in surprise, he dropped his hand back to his side.

"It was that 'knocked up and abandoned' comment that got to me," he said flatly. "That was a lousy thing for her to say to you."

Prudence sighed philosophically. "Yeah, well, here's a news flash, Dr. Mahoney. In case you haven't heard, I *was* knocked up and abandoned. That's the whole point. Hazel's right. Everybody in high school was right. I'm totally irresponsible."

He eyed her with much speculation, noting the rigid set to her shoulders, her stiff spine and her uplifted chin. She looked as if she were preparing for battle. Although he couldn't quite disagree with her claim, very softly, he asked, "Are you? Irresponsible, I mean?"

She nodded vigorously. "Oh, yeah. Weren't you listening?"

He nodded back, though much more slowly and thoughtfully than she had. "Yes, as a matter of fact, I was. And that wasn't what I got from the conversation at all."

"Then what did you get?"

Instead of answering her, he only smiled a knowing little smile. Then after a moment he said, "So. We're going to this reunion as husband and wife. Something tells me we should prepare."

Her eyebrows arched so high they disappeared completely beneath her bangs. "We don't have to prepare anything," she assured him.

"Why not?"

"Because we're not going, that's why."

Feeling completely affronted for some reason, Seth repeated, "Why not?"

She gaped at him. "Because we're not husband and wife, that's why not."

He shrugged off her concern quite literally. "A minor detail."

"A *major* detail," she corrected him. "You just invented a life for me that's a complete lie. I can't go to the reunion now. I'd never be able to pull it off. It's bad enough that Hazel is going to be telling everyone I'm living the way you described. If *I* go, and then let everyone think what she said is true, that would just make me as big a liar as...as...as..."

"As I am?" he supplied helpfully.

She lifted one shoulder and let it drop. "Well..." she said.

But she never finished the statement. Probably, Seth thought, because she didn't think it was necessary.

"Look, Prudence," he said. "Let me explain something to you here. It is absolutely essential for one to go to one's high school reunion."

"Why?" she asked.

Without hesitation he told her, "To get even."

She gaped at him again. "Well, that's a terrible thing to say."

"It's also true," he assured her. "Come on, don't get all noble on me. Nobility is so incredibly tedious."

"I'm not being noble, I'm just being…"

"What?"

"Decent," she said.

He shuddered. "Being decent is even worse than being noble. Do not go there. More important, do not take me there with you. Let *me* take *you* someplace instead." He tried—but not very hard—to keep the lasciviousness out of his voice as he added, "Someplace where you'll have a very good time."

She narrowed her eyes at him suspiciously.

"No, not *that* someplace," he told her with what he hoped was a sly and salacious look. "Although, if you're ever interested, I certainly wouldn't mind giving you a tour of each and every attraction to be found at that particular someplace, too…"

She narrowed her eyes at him even more. She also, he was pretty sure, growled at him under her breath.

Seth sighed dramatically. "I meant a different someplace."

Prudence hesitated a moment before saying, "I don't understand."

Seth grinned. "Let me take you to your class reunion," he told her. "As your husband and Tanner's father."

She shook her head vehemently. "Absolutely not."

"Prudence."

When she heard the way he said her name, involuntarily she clammed up and lifted her head to meet his gaze.

"Trust me on this," he told her. "You need to go to this reunion, and you need to do it to show everyone up."

"But that's just the point, Dr. Mahoney. I can't show them up. I turned out exactly the way they all knew I would. All it would wind up being is an I-told-you-so fest for everyone else, and utter humiliation for me."

"Not if I'm with you, it wouldn't."

"You won't be with me," she told him.

"Why not?"

"Because I'm not going."

"But—"

"In fact," she said, "as it stands, I'm going to have to call Hazel and tell her the truth about...you and me... before *she* goes to the reunion."

Seth couldn't believe what he was hearing. After all he'd done to get her out of her jam, this was the way she thanked him. Him. Dr. Seth Mahoney. Knight in shining armor. "Why would you need to do that?" he demanded.

"Because it's bad enough that *one* person in my senior class has been misinformed," she told him. "If Hazel goes to the reunion, she'll tell everybody what you just said about me. What you said about—" she met his gaze nervously "—about...us."

"And the problem with that would be...?" he asked.

"That it's a big, fat lie."

"And the problem with that would be...?"

"Dr. Mahoney!" she exclaimed, her exasperation with him more than evident.

"Seth," he automatically corrected her. "How many times do I have to tell you to call me Seth? You're the only one in neurology who still calls me Dr. Mahoney—or Dr. Insufferable, whatever—and seeing as how I've just made you my wife, the least you could do is address me by my first name. Though if you want to call me 'darling,' that would be all right, too."

She didn't look amused.

"Fine," he said. "Call Witch Hazel and tell her the truth. But don't come crying to me when she makes you feel like a...like a..."

"Like a complete loser in the game of life?" Prudence finished for him.

Seth's shoulders slumped in defeat. "No, Prudence. That's not what I was going to say."

"Funny," she replied, "because that's exactly what I feel like."

Before he could contradict her, she scooped up the file lying on the counter before her and tried to push past him. Unsure why he did it, Seth snaked out a hand and circled her wrist with a grip that surprised even him, halting her before she could get away. And as much as he really wanted to tug hard on her hand and haul her entire body alongside his, somehow he refrained from doing so.

"You're not a loser," he stated unequivocally.

She pulled halfheartedly at his grasp. "Please let me go."

"Not until I know you're okay."

"I'm okay."

"Sure you are."

"I am."

"Prudence."

She still didn't look at him, but she said, "What?"

Seth opened his mouth to speak, then realized belatedly that he had no idea what he had intended to tell her. So he only said, "I'm sorry if I made things worse for you than they already were. I was just trying to help."

She did look at him then, and for some reason her expression was so sad. But she only shrugged softly and said, "That's okay. For a few minutes, there, I was kind of enjoying myself. That's more time than I ever got in high school."

Seth wanted to tell her that he could relate, but the words got stuck somewhere inside him. So he released her wrist and let her go and tried not to think about how lonely it felt standing there at the nurses' station—or anywhere else on the planet, for that matter—without her.

Four

Exactly one week after Seth Mahoney had made her his wife whether she'd liked it or not—and, increasingly, distressingly, Pru had discovered that she did sort of like it—she was right back where she started from. As she sat at the nurses' station in neurology, she felt much as she had last week, the afternoon Seth had misrepresented their marital status for Hazel—as if the surreal had replaced the real in her reality, making it surreality.

Or something like that.

Instead of being filled with energy, as she usually was when she arrived at work, today Pru sat hunched over the counter with her head cradled in both hands. An evil headache sliced open her brain, and any minute now she was sure she was going to lose what little breakfast she had managed to ingest that morning.

Boy, who knew how guilt and shame and fear and panic could wreak such havoc with a person's system?

The night before she had finally tracked down a telephone number for Hazel Dubrowski Debbit in Pittsburgh, had finally gotten to speak to her former classmate about the misconception Seth had fed her the week before over their state of nonexistent wedded bliss. She'd called Hazel to come clean with the truth, to set things right, to apologize and explain and try to make amends. But before she'd had a chance to do any of those things, Hazel had blurted out a pretty surprising announcement of her own.

Gosh, she had said, she hoped Pru didn't mind, but she hadn't been able to keep the news of Pru's new life to herself, and she'd called everyone—just *everyone,* darling—in Easton High's class of '90 to tell them the news. That Prudence Holloway, voted "Most Irresponsible," had, in fact become the most upright, responsible woman in the world, marrying a steady, rich—and just too, too gorgeous—doctor.

"Ohhhh…" Pru groaned softly to herself now as the memory swirled through her brain.

Hazel had filled *everyone* in on the details of Pru's fake life, had told them *all* about the big house, the subscriptions to the arts, the volunteer work, the beautiful bouncing baby boy. And now *everyone* just couldn't wait to see Pru and her beautiful, upright, responsible family at the reunion. They were *all* just so excited about her life-affirming transformation.

In response to this new development, and to her utter horror, Pru had found herself holding the receiver in a white-knuckled grip, unable to refute a word of it. She had sat silent and openmouthed as she listened to Hazel's incessant chattering, had shaken her head in numb disbelief. The few times Pru had tried to interrupt and make a half-hearted effort to clarify things, Hazel had erupted in another long monologue about how great it was going to be to see everyone's expression when they realized the truth about Pru.

The truth about Pru.

"Ohhhh..." she groaned again.

Who did she think she was? she demanded of herself for perhaps the hundredth time since hanging up the telephone the night before without correcting Hazel's misconceptions. How could she keep perpetuating a lie she should have corrected a week ago, a lie she never should have allowed in the first place? What was she going to do now? When was she going to learn? Where was she going to find the strength to tell Hazel the truth about the heinous thing she had let happen?

Only someone who was completely irresponsible would have let things go this far.

"Why, Prudence. Just the delectable little morsel I've been looking for."

And how could she get Dr. Mahoney to stop calling her by her given name? Not only did she not particularly care for it, but every time someone called her that, it only served to remind her how very *im*prudent she had been all her life.

More than any of the other questions uncoiling in her brain today, however, one in particular assaulted her. Namely, why did her body turn into a hot, shuddering mass of Jell-O every time Dr. Mahoney came within fifty feet of her? She could feel herself melting and quivering already. It made no sense. There was absolutely no reason for her to be as attracted to him as she was, as she had been for two years. None. Nada. Zip. Zilch.

Okay, except maybe for the fact that he was really handsome. That *might* be a reason. Fine. She could live with that. Or maybe because he was so charming. That, too, could explain her fascination with him. And he was funny. Yes, that factor, as well, was perfectly understandable. And yes, there was the fact that he was kind of...sort of...okay, incredibly...sexy.

But *lots* of guys were handsome, charming, funny and sexy. That still didn't provide her with a sound, rational explanation for why, every time Dr. Mahoney came around, she wanted to hurl herself into his arms, wrap her legs around his torso and feed herself to him in one, big bite.

"Ohhhh…"

And on top of that, she now had those two brief kisses he had bestowed upon her the week before to think back on. And, boy, had she thought back on them. A lot. And every time she did, a strange heat began circling in the pit of her stomach, and all kinds of unthinkable ideas began unrolling in her brain.

Boy, was she irresponsible, to have fallen for a guy like him. Thank goodness for Tanner, she thought. Because although she might have acted rashly in conceiving her son— and in a lot of other things in her past—she'd certainly grown up since having him. Okay, so maybe she wasn't the most responsible person in the world, she conceded. At least she knew better than to act on her impulses where Dr. Mahoney was concerned.

Now if she could just do something about that big, fat, whopping lie they'd told to Hazel…

"Ohhhh…"

"Prudence? Are you…all right?"

At Seth Mahoney's softly uttered question, she only nodded mutely. Then she shook off her anxieties—all twelve hundred of them—and reminded herself that she *had* been trying, very hard, to be responsible since Tanner's birth. And many times—at least five—she had succeeded.

She didn't make a single decision these days without considering her child's welfare first. There was no way she would ever compromise her baby boy. Pru lived her life in a perfectly responsible fashion now—well, except for that, you know, big, fat, whopping lie to which she had recently been accessory. And it was all thanks to Tanner's appearance in her life.

Of course, Tanner's appearance in her life also meant she hadn't had a single date with anyone since he was conceived, which, now that she thought more about it, might go a long way toward explaining all that leg-wrapping, feeding-herself-to-Dr. Mahoney-in-one-big-bite business.

Once again, Pru shoved the thought away and focused instead on not bashing her forehead against the counter of the nurses' station in frustration. Dr. Mahoney was staring at her in a way that required a response. So she took a deep breath and forced herself to meet his gaze as levelly as she could.

Ohh, bad move, she decided immediately. Because, as always, the moment she looked into his eyes, she felt herself drowning in their blue, blue depths.

"Good morning," he said, smiling sweetly, as if their intimate little conspiracy of the week before had never occurred. As if there were no heated energy burning up the air between them. As if her entire body wasn't humming with awareness just because he'd come within ten feet of her. As if the angels hadn't risen in chorus above, and all the planets hadn't harmonically converged, simply because he existed in the universe.

Get a grip, Pru. You'll embarrass yourself.

"Morning," she replied, willing to concede at least the last part of his observation. As unobtrusively as she could, she swiped a hand across her chin, just in case she had been drooling.

"My, but you're looking particularly ravishing today," he cooed. Actually cooed. Amazing. What was even more amazing was that Pru found herself falling for it. Because behind her rib cage, she could just feel her heart going, *putt-putt-putt-putt-putt...varoooooom.*

Oh, no. Not again.

"Uh...thanks," she said. And then, although she had no

idea what possessed her to do it, she added, "You're looking rather, um…dapper?…yourself."

She might as well have just told him he was the winner of the Publisher's Clearinghouse Giveaway, because the expression that crossed his face then was radiant. Truly radiant. For all of four or five seconds. Then immediately that radiance fled. In its place his expression darkened thunderously.

"Just what the hell did you mean by that?" he demanded.

Pru arched her brows at his abrupt turnabout. "What do you mean, what did I mean?"

He, in turn, narrowed his eyes at her. "You just paid me a compliment, dammit. And I demand to know the reason why."

She gaped in surprise. "You act like I insulted you."

"No, you *didn't* insult me. That's just the problem."

Pru was sure she misunderstood. "It's a problem that I *didn't* insult you?"

He nodded stiffly. "When you insult me, I know where I stand with you, Prudence, but a compliment…?"

"A compliment?" she prodded.

"Well, it was entirely uncalled for, that's all."

"Oh. Uh…sorry?"

He nodded slowly, warily. "Just don't let it happen again."

"O-okay."

Now that she thought about it, Pru had to admit that she, too, was surprised by the fact that she had said something nice to Dr. Mahoney. Even though she always *thought* he looked dapper—or ravishing, or delectable, or…oh, never mind—she never actually *told* him such a thing. She never told him about *any* of the things she felt whenever she saw him. She couldn't. It would be much too dangerous to put voice to those thoughts, those feelings, and have him know where he stood with her.

Because if Dr. Mahoney knew about the stir of warm, raucous sensations he roused in her, then he might think she was interested in him. There was no way she would ever risk letting him find out about that interest. There was no way she would ever risk acting on her interest, either. It would only serve to make things far too interesting. And that was something she simply could not afford.

The last thing Pru needed was to have him keep asking her out again, the way he had for so long after his arrival at Seton General. It had been exhausting trying to maintain her distance, had been nearly impossible to keep from succumbing to his numerous—and, she recalled with a wistful smile, very persuasive—efforts to charm her. Especially since all she'd really wanted to do was succumb to him. Over and over again. Preferably in a horizontal fashion.

But she'd known right off the bat that he was the last man she should succumb to, horizontally *or* vertically. He was Dr. Irresistible, after all. He changed women more frequently than a leopard changed its spots.

Or something like that.

Anyway, the point was, she didn't need to be sitting here saying nice things to Seth Mahoney, because it would only encourage him to say nice things back to her. And if he started saying nice things back to her, then she couldn't be held responsible for her actions. Because, hey, she was totally irresponsible. She had documented evidence to prove that in her high school yearbook.

And who did she think she was, anyway, paying him compliments? she wondered further, her brain—along with other body parts—obviously not quite willing to let go of him just yet. It was as if she was trying to butter him up or something. As if she was about to ask him for a favor and wanted to put him in the best possible frame of mind first, so that he'd be less likely to turn her down. As if she planned to make a request of him that he might not be willing to go along with unless he were feeling flattered and obligated to her somehow. As if she honestly had it in her mind to ask him to—

Uh-oh.

Oh, no, she thought. *Oh, no, please. Not that. Anything but that.*

She couldn't possibly be considering such a thing. She couldn't possibly be planning to perpetuate the lie they had told to Hazel. She couldn't possibly be thinking that she could keep up with this stupid charade of being blissfully married and totally responsible. She couldn't possibly be considering asking Seth Mahoney to accompany her to Pittsburgh next month, to pose as her husband and the father of her child.

Could she?

Oh, no. Oh, no, please. Not that. Anything but that.

Seth couldn't quite believe that Prudence Holloway was looking at him the way she was looking at him—as if she had every intention of leaping over the nurse's station to wrap her legs around his waist and…and…and…

No way. She couldn't possibly be planning to do *that.*

Could she?

He shook his head once, to clear it of the errant—though not altogether unpleasant—idea. And he wondered why he had just thrown Prudence Holloway's compliment back in her face so shabbily the way he had, especially since there was little chance he'd ever be receiving one from her again.

It had just come as such a surprise, that was all. He couldn't remember the last time she'd said something nice to him. In fact, now that he gave it more consideration, he didn't think she'd *ever* said anything nice to him. Well, not until their little…whatever that had been between them and

Witch Hazel last week. And now he'd just made certain she would never say anything nice to him again.

Unbelievable, he thought. He—*he,* Dr. Seth Mahoney, pleasure seeker—had just blown any potential for actually *finding* pleasure where Prudence Holloway was concerned.

Damn, damn and double damn.

"Uh, Dr. Mahoney?"

There was something about the soft timbre of her voice that twisted a knot tight inside him, and Seth couldn't quite help himself when he took the single—giant—step necessary to close the distance between himself and the nurses' station. He folded one arm flat over the counter, levered the other to prop his chin in his palm, then shifted his weight to one foot, thereby striking what he hoped was a roguish, yet not unappealing, pose.

"Yes, Prudence?" he replied.

She blinked once, and he homed in on the way her pupils expanded slightly for just an infinitesimal moment before contracting once again. Good God, her eyes were green.

"Um," she said softly, "could I, uh…could I…talk…to you…about something?"

Well, that sounded rather intriguing. Mostly because when she said it her eyes darkened curiously and her expression shifted to one of total uncertainty.

"Sure," he said. "You can talk to me about anything."

She licked her lips anxiously, and Seth inevitably dropped his gaze to her mouth. Not a good idea, he decided immediately. Because Prudence Holloway had the kind of mouth that caused a man many a sleepless night. He knew that for a fact. Because in the past two years he'd lost quite a bit of sleep thinking about that mouth.

About that lush, ripe, delicious-looking mouth. About how it would feel, soft and yielding, under his. About how it would look, slightly open as a result of her unutterable passion. About how it would taste when he traced the out-

line with his tongue. About the soft sighs it would emit as
he did things to the rest of her body that were doubtless
illegal in the state of New Jersey.

As Seth's thoughts started to get away from him, he
shifted his weight to the other foot, hoping to alleviate some
of the pressure that was building up in his groin. Yeah,
Prudence Holloway had some mouth on her, all right. He
just wished he could come up with a way to get it on him,
too.

She leaned forward a bit before speaking again, and instinctively Seth followed suit, bringing his own head down
until it nearly touched hers. Lowering her voice to a conspiratorial murmur, she asked, "Can I…can I talk to you
about something…personal?"

Oh, now this was *definitely* sounding intriguing. And her
mouth was *definitely* looking more appealing. "Oh, by all
means," he assured her.

She hesitated only a moment before continuing, even
more softly, "Right now?"

Seth hoped he didn't look too eager as he nodded
quickly. Several times. "Absolutely."

"Alone?"

Instead of offering a verbal reply this time, Seth nodded
once more—very fast—and pivoted on his heel so quickly
that he nearly spun right down the hall. Then he was off
like a shot, hoping like hell that Prudence could keep up
with him, because he couldn't *wait* to get alone with her
to discuss this personal matter that she had to discuss with
him personally. Him. Dr. Seth Mahoney. Coveter of all
things Prudence. Without looking back, he headed for a
storage closet he knew well, pushed the door open, thrust
himself inside, flipped on the light and waited.

He didn't have to wait long.

Because within seconds Prudence barreled in right behind him, looking confused, agitated and not a little flus-

tered. And Seth decided very quickly that when Prudence was flustered, she looked quite…fetching. And her mouth looked quite…luscious. And he just couldn't wait to see if she tasted that way, too.

The moment she was inside the closet with him, he let the door swing closed behind her on a nearly silent *swoosh*. And then, very much unable to help himself, he pulled her into his arms, pressed her back against the door and then crowded his body into hers.

Arcing one arm over her head to place it firmly against the door, he smiled and said, "We have *got* to stop meeting like this." Then he bent his head down to hers and kissed her.

He didn't know why. He just did. He couldn't help himself. She was irresistible.

He waited for her to shove him backward with all her might, as she had done the last time he'd dared to hem her in this way. But much to his surprise—not to mention his delight—this time, for one brief, delirious moment Prudence didn't push him away. In fact, this time, for one brief, delirious moment Prudence kissed him back. With gusto.

She roped one arm around his waist and cupped the other over his shoulder, then tilted her head to the side to receive his kiss fully. Immediately he took liberties with the embrace, rubbing his mouth faintly over hers, tracing her plump lower lip with the tip of his tongue before delving inside for a more complete taste of her. Prudence sighed at his intrusion, opening her mouth in invitation. And Seth was only too happy to RSVP.

Deepening the kiss, he dropped one hand to her hip, flattening his palm against the soft fabric of her scrubs as he began to rub it along her thigh. Over and over, up and down, he caressed her, until he could feel the friction of heat building beneath his hand. Then he unfolded his fingers over the elegant curve of her hip, scooping further back to push his fingertips into the taut lower curve of her bottom.

Oh, she felt...*so* good.

She must have been thinking the same thing about him, because, somehow, Seth registered the warmth of her palm as it curled around his nape, and the brush of her fingers as they sifted gingerly through his hair. He felt the rapid-fire thumping of her heart against his, noted the way her chest rose and fell raggedly as she, too, tried to catch her breath.

But it was the heat that nearly did him in. The coils of frantic energy that sizzled and arced between them were a thing of wonder he figured he probably shouldn't think too much about right now. So instead of thinking, Seth acted. And in that single moment of unbridled passion, as he held Prudence close and touched her in all those ways—and all those places—he had always wanted to touch her, as he tasted her over and over again, he got the ride of his life.

Unfortunately for him, however, that ride was *very* short-lived.

Because as hastily and as easily as she had surrendered to him, Prudence suddenly began to wage war. Just as Seth was beginning to feel as if nothing in his life could ever go wrong again, just as he was becoming certain that he'd found his niche, right here in the arms of Nurse Irresistible, just as he became convinced that he was right where he wanted to be for the rest of his natural life, he found himself...

...elsewhere.

Namely, flat on his fanny in the middle of the storage closet, where he landed when Prudence came to her senses and shoved him away. Hard.

Ohh, he was really starting to dislike the way she did that.

The last time she had reacted in such a manner, Seth had

been prepared for it—well, sort of prepared, anyway—because he'd known she wouldn't tolerate his advances. That last time he'd been able to recover his balance before he went sprawling. This time, however, he'd been just a *tad* preoccupied with other things. So Prudence's reaction had come as something of a surprise. And it had been much more effective in catching him off guard. And off foot, too.

For a long moment, Seth could only sit there on his indignity, staring up at her with his mouth agape. How could he—*he,* Dr. Seth Mahoney, grace under fire—have ended up in such an ignoble position? More important than that, however, how was he going to get Prudence back where he wanted her?

Because one thing became crystal clear to Seth in that moment as he sat gazing up at her: he had never, ever, wanted a woman the way he wanted Prudence Holloway. And whatever it took to have her, *whatever it took,* he would do it.

He would have her.

Exactly where he wanted her.

Just…later, he thought as he noted again his less-than-imposing position on the floor.

"All right, I guess I deserved that," he said, folding his legs up before him, looping his arms casually around his knees. "But I *won't* apologize for something I should have done a long time ago."

With as much dignity as he could muster—which, granted, under the circumstances, wasn't much—he pushed himself up off the floor. Then, with as much casualness as he could rouse—which, again, wasn't much—he brushed off his khaki trousers, his Tasmanian Devil necktie and his white doctor jacket. Then he craned his neck and rolled his shoulders, as if what had just happened was in no way out of the ordinary for him.

But it was, of course, completely out of the ordinary.

Women never discouraged him. They never pushed him away. And they never stared at him with eyes so wide and stricken that he felt as if he'd just plucked off their wings.

When he looked at Prudence, however, he realized that this was a first for her, too. Her eyes were filled with something akin to panic, and she had the back of one hand pressed lightly against her mouth. Somehow, though, he couldn't quite say for sure whether she was trying to wipe off the remnants of his touch, or attempting to preserve the sensation forever.

"Why...why did you do that?" she demanded, the question coming out muffled, thanks to that hand-over-the-mouth business. "Why did you...kiss me that way?"

Seth forced a jocularity into his voice he was nowhere close to feeling. "That way? Well, that particular kiss— number seven, don't you know—just so happens to be the best way I know how," he quipped. "Of course, I know lots of other ways, too. If you liked that one, then maybe we could try number three next. It's a doozy."

She obviously didn't get the joke, because she didn't alter her position or expression at all. "But *why* did you do it?" she demanded.

He eyed her narrowly. "Why did you let me?"

She shook her head softly. "I didn't—"

"You did," he quickly cut her off. "You did, and you know it."

This time she didn't deny it, only widened her eyes in surprise, as if just now realizing how very willing a participant she had been. For a few minutes, anyway. Okay, one minute, he amended reluctantly. But she *had* been a willing participant. Heat stirred in his midsection again when he recalled just how willing.

"Don't do that to me ever again," she told him as she dropped her hand back to her side.

"Why not?" he asked flatly, stung by the vehemence of

her command. "You seemed to be enjoying yourself as much as I was enjoying yourself."

She started to shake her head again, seemed to think better of it and said, "I just don't want you to do it. Ever again."

Seth inhaled a slow, steadying breath, and released it just as leisurely. "Then tell me, Prudence, my lovely, my sweet. What is it that you *do* want? I seem to recall something of a deep, personal nature that you needed to discuss with me—*alone*. Just what is it, exactly, that you wanted?"

She swallowed hard, but her eyes were still wide and frightened, and she was still obviously not thinking clearly, when she said, "I want...I want you..." But her voice trailed off before she finished.

Hope flickered to life inside Seth. "You want me?" he asked, taking a step toward her. "Well, you certainly have a funny way of showing it. Why, Prudence, you need only but ask. I'm yours for the taking. I thought I made that clear a long time ago."

She shook her head hard. "No, that's not what I meant. I mean, I do want you..."

He arched an eyebrow quizzically.

"I mean, I need you..."

The other eyebrow followed suit.

"That is..." She swallowed hard again, then sighed fitfully.

"Like I said, Prudence, I'm yours for the taking. Just tell me how you want me." He couldn't quite keep himself from adding, "And do be specific. I'm not at all put off by unconventional positions. On the contrary."

She screwed up her features as if she was having trouble trying to put voice to whatever it was she was trying to tell him, but wanted desperately to say something, if for no other reason than to simply shut him up. Finally she inhaled a deep breath, swallowed hard and released it slowly.

"You don't understand," she said.

"Then explain it to me," he told her. "I'm trying, Prudence, really I am. But you're not making it easy."

She inhaled one more breath, and as she released it on a rush of words, she told him, "I want you—need you—to be my husband."

Five

Okay, Seth thought as panic clawed at the back of his throat. This could mean one of two things. Either Prudence was referring to their little charade of a week ago, when they'd pretended to be blissfully wed for the benefit of Witch Hazel or...

...or not.

Oh, surely this was related to that charade business, he told himself. After all these months of avoiding him, there was no way Prudence could be proposing to him. After just pushing him away—hard—it was unthinkable that she could be offering him the position of fatherhood where her baby son was concerned. After commanding him to never, ever, kiss her again, she couldn't honestly be suggesting that he—*he,* Dr. Seth Mahoney, confirmed bachelor—become Mr. Prudence Holloway.

Could she?

Oh, he didn't *think* so.

Not only was her question completely at odds with her behavior, but there was no way he—*he*, Dr. Seth Mahoney, lovable rogue—would ever commit himself to one woman. Or one child. Or one long-distance carrier, for that matter.

On the heels of his absolute conviction, however, he was surprised by another consideration. The consideration that maybe, just maybe, life as Mr. Prudence Holloway might not be such a bad gig at that. Then, immediately on the heels of *that* thought, he told himself he was crazy for thinking such a thing. He was Dr. Irresistible, after all. Not Dr. Husband. And certainly not Dr. Daddy.

"You, uh…you want me to be *what?*" he asked.

This time Prudence was the one to shake her head, a bit more vigorously than he had himself earlier. Then again, he thought, if her proposal was actually valid, then she had a hell of a lot more cluttering up her head this morning than he did. Like maybe rocks, for instance.

"I'm sorry," she said quickly. "That came out all wrong."

"Well, I should hope so."

She studied him in silence for a long time, until Seth started feeling like a lab specimen. A lab specimen that was about to become a lab experiment, at that. He steeled himself for the worst, then realized he didn't want to envision what the worst might be.

Finally Prudence told him, "What I meant was that I want you to *pretend* to be my husband. For the reunion. Next month."

Oh, was *that* all? he thought.

"So I see you've come to your senses about that," he said, marveling at the thread of relief that wound through him. Then he wondered why *he* should be the one feeling relieved. It was *her* neck that was in the noose. Granted, he had been the one to put it there, but that was beside the point.

"So then your offer is still good?" she asked. Something in her voice, though, suggested that she was hoping he'd turn her down.

Not. Bloody. Likely.

"Of course the offer is still good," he assured her.

"Great," she said blandly.

"It's a dirty job to be sure," he added, "but someone's got to do it. And, Prudence, if you must be getting dirty with someone, well…it might as well be me. I have experience in this sort of thing. You won't be sorry."

She gulped visibly at his response and said, "Uh…"

But she never expanded on that particular remark, seeing as how the door behind her was pushed open from the other side, a development for which she was obviously unprepared. Because as the door whacked her softly on the backside, Prudence went careering forward…right back into Seth's arms.

He decided to take it as a sign.

The nurse who entered the storage closet, on the other hand, clearly decided to take it as a bit of fodder for the ol' rumor mill. Because all she did was smile sweetly and murmur a soft "Excuse me," then turn right back around and exit as stealthily and unexpectedly as she had entered.

Before Prudence had a chance to pull away from him, Seth tugged her close, wrapping both arms loosely around her waist. He didn't want to risk a back injury by kissing her again, but he sure as hell knew enough to take advantage of a situation when it presented itself this way.

"Better get used to it, Mrs. Mahoney," he said. "From this day forward, until the end of next month, anyway, we're man and wife. To have—" he tightened his arms just a tad "—and to hold."

"For better or for worse," she threw in halfheartedly.

"To honor and obey," he added with a leering smile.

"Oh, I don't know about *that*…"

"Whatever. At any rate, we'd better get used to each other if we're going to convince others that we're married. That we've been married long enough to produce a bouncing baby boy. Besides," he said, thinking about the nurse who had just discovered them, "that was Melody Applebaum who just walked in on us. The mouth that roared. It looks like we're about to become an item here at Seton, anyway. Whether we like it or not."

He could see quite clearly by the expression on Prudence's face that she did not like it at all. Seth, however...

Well, he was going to reserve judgment for now. There was just no telling what a weekend in Pittsburgh might bring.

Pru inhaled a deep, calming breath as she gazed at the tiny table in her tiny dining room, thinking it looked very strange set for two. Tanner's high chair was placed in its usual spot, but its usual spot, instead of just being next to Pru, was now in between Pru and what would be Seth Mahoney's seat at the table.

Seth Mahoney's seat at the table, she repeated to herself as a banner of anxiety unfurled in her belly. Now there was a phrase she'd never thought to use in relation to her home. And even though she'd had a week to get used to the *idea* of being married to him—fictionally, of course—they hadn't yet practiced the physical aspect.

Not that she was honestly planning to practice the physical aspect of marriage. At least, not that...you know... *particular* physical aspect. But they needed to start feeling more comfortable with each other, because they would have to effortlessly exchange all those little touches and gestures of affection that came so naturally to married couples. And the best way to accomplish being comfortable together was to spend more time together. Physically. Not that Pru was planning on exchanging a lot of those little touches and gestures. No way. But mastering one or two of them would probably be a good idea. Or maybe three or four. Or ten or twelve. She'd have to see how things went.

In any case, they had both decided it would be a good idea to spend more time together, so that they could become more familiar with each other, before undertaking what she had come to term the Pittsburgh Project.

Undertaking, she reflected. Not a good word to use in regard to this thing. Because the way she was beginning to feel about it all, she suspected she was going to need an undertaker before it was over.

She still wasn't sure what had possessed her to ask Seth Mahoney—Dr. Irresistible—to help her perpetuate a lie she should have rectified the minute it entered the world. Desperation, she immediately answered herself. That's what had come over her. Hearing Hazel go on about how she had informed their entire senior class of Pru's new life-style—Pru's totally fictitious, impossible-to-explain-without-being-utterly-humiliated lifestyle—she'd just snapped. And now there were only three weeks to go until her reunion, three weeks for her to get used to the idea of Seth Mahoney being her husband. Her husband and Tanner's father.

Her gaze fell to the baby boy who sat in the attached living room amid a scattering of bright plastic toys. As if he knew he was the topic of Pru's thoughts, he turned to look at his mother and smiled that broad, toothless smile that always brought a grin—and a ripple of unmitigated adoration—from her.

With his dark hair and green eyes, he bore a striking resemblance to her, something for which she was daily grateful. Not just because she didn't need any added reminders of Kevin haunting her for the rest of her life, but because, quite frankly, her features were much more nicely arranged than his were anyway. And, of course, it would also come in handy now, because nobody at the reunion would look at Tanner and wonder about his paternity.

Oh, God. She wished she could stop thinking about *everything* in terms of her high school reunion. It was as if the event were turning into some unmanageable beast that would be consuming her whole. It was just a reunion, she reminded herself. A bunch of people she hadn't seen for ten years. A bunch of people who'd made her life anything but enjoyable to begin with. So why was she so worried about what they thought of her now?

She was no closer to an answer to that this evening than she had been ten years ago. Pru had no idea why it was so important to her that she go to this reunion as an upright, forthright, do right kind of person, instead of wearing the perpetual label of "Most Irresponsible" that she would doubtless take to her grave, anyway. It was just that she had been the butt of too many jokes over the years, had spent too much of her youth being jeered at and ridiculed. Just once in her life, she wanted to see what it felt like to be thought of as something other than a laughingstock.

Even if a laughingstock was exactly what she continued to be these days. As evidenced by this latest fiasco of wanting to pretend to be something she wasn't. Oh, why didn't she have the backbone to just call Hazel Dubrowski Debbit and explain things and get it over with? Who cared if her senior class spent the entire weekend making fun of the situation? she asked herself. If she told Hazel the truth, Pru wouldn't be at the reunion, anyway. So what difference did it make if they were still laughing at her after all this time?

She honestly couldn't answer that question. All she knew was that it *did* make a difference. She didn't want to be laughed at anymore. Maybe, the way so many other things in her life were these days, it was for Tanner's sake. She wanted to be a good mother. She wanted to be a good provider, a good role model, a good influence. And somehow, as long as she wore the mantle of "Most Irresponsible," she felt like none of those things. Tanner's very existence in the world was evidence of her irresponsible behavior, and she wanted to make up to him for that. She wanted the rest of his life to be perfect and free of any stigma.

And although she knew creating a perfect life for him would be impossible, regardless of the kind of person she was, allowing this little charade at her reunion would be one less blemish attached to Tanner's existence. Even if it was a complete farce.

Somehow, the explanation made sense to Pru, and she took comfort in it, however lame it might be. If things worked out the way they were supposed to, no one at the reunion would ever be the wiser regarding Tanner's paternity—or her own irresponsibility. In ten years she could go to her twenty-year reunion without Seth Mahoney, pose as a divorced woman and not be at all out of place. Well, except, of course, for being a big, fat liar.

But, hey, nobody was perfect.

The rough grating of the doorbell jerked Pru out of her ruminations and had Tanner rolling over onto all fours so that he could crawl to greet the newcomer. He got more excited than a spaniel when someone came to call, and was always there to greet whomever arrived for a visit. Pru just hoped he hit it off well with Seth Mahoney. Because Dr. Irresistible was going to be his daddy for a while. And her husband, too.

Inhaling another deep breath to calm herself, Pru swept a hand down the long, loose lavender sweater she'd donned over matching leggings, then bent to pick up Tanner, who looked very dapper in a bright-blue romper. She snuggled him close, nuzzling the sweet baby smell of his neck, then smiled at his chuckle as she reached for the doorknob.

And then she almost fainted when she saw Dr. Mahoney standing on the other side. She was used to seeing him in his doctor duds of trousers, button-down shirts and ties. She'd never laid eyes on him when he was wearing form-fitting, lovingly faded Levi's and a baggy sweater that had probably once been a rich indigo-blue, but which had softened over washings so that it was now almost the same color as his jeans. And now that she did lay eyes on him this way, she realized she wanted to lay other body parts on him, too. In fact, she realized, she wanted to lay her entire body on him. And she wondered if maybe, if she was very, very good, he would return the favor soon.

He smiled mischievously when he saw her expression, as if he knew perfectly well what she was thinking about, and that yes, by all means, he'd be more than happy to return the favor soon. Several times over, if possible.

Then, very softly, he said, "Hi, honey. I'm home."

To punctuate the statement, he bent forward and brushed a soft kiss over her cheek, then pulled back carelessly, as if the transaction were something the two of them shared every day. Too stunned to say anything in response, Pru only gasped softly and pressed her fingertips lightly to her heated face, in exactly the spot he had touched with his mouth. Somehow she garnered the nerve to meet his gaze, and then melted a little inside when she saw the fire that ignited in the dangerous depths of his blue, blue eyes.

"For you," he said softly, extending a bouquet of daisies and carnations toward her.

Although she loathed the thought of dropping her hand from the still-tingling cheek he had kissed, Pru reached out to take them from him. She noted then that he had a bottle of wine tucked under one arm, and she was grateful for its arrival. She rarely bought wine these days—it was beyond her budget, and she liked to keep her wits about her now that she was a mother—but she suspected she was going to need something to steady her pulse this evening. It was already accelerating dangerously past the speed limit.

"Wow, Tanner's gotten big," Dr. Mahoney said as he released the bouquet to her care. "I haven't seen him for a while. It's amazing how fast they grow, isn't it?"

Pru narrowed her eyes suspiciously. "You seem to know an awful lot about it. Do you…have one or two of you own?"

He chuckled, but his attention was focused on Tanner instead of Pru. "No," he told her. "I don't have any kids. But I do like them."

"That doesn't surprise me," she replied.

"Why not?"

She opened her mouth to offer a quip about how it was because he seemed to have so much in common with them, then decided to keep it to herself. He was doing her a favor. There was no reason for her to deride him. Even if he *did* behave like a child most of the time.

Stop it, Pru. He's doing something nice for you. The least you can do is be nice back. "You, uh…you just seem like the kind of guy who would like kids, that's all," she finally told him.

When he turned his head from Tanner to look at her, she could tell by his expression that he knew what she had been thinking. He didn't call her on it, however, and only smiled that mouth-watering, heat-inducing, libido-scrambling smile of his.

"Uh, come on in," she said, stepping aside so that he could do just that. Tanner had already gone after one of the daisies in the bouquet and was plucking it apart petal by petal. Pru pulled it out of his reach and tried to balance both baby and flowers, not really managing either very well.

"Here, let me," Dr. Mahoney said.

But instead of reaching for the bouquet, which she had

expected him to do, he held out his hands toward Tanner.
And Tanner, the little traitor, went quite willingly into their
guest's arms. Pru caught the bottle of wine as he went, and
then she and Seth Mahoney had effectively, and completely, traded places.

Well, this was certainly an interesting development, she
thought. As much as Tanner enjoyed greeting visitors, he
didn't normally warm up to guests very quickly. Even with
people she knew well, her son generally needed a good fif-
teen or twenty minutes before he would go willingly into
their care. Something about Seth Mahoney clearly spoke to
the little guy, though.

As she watched the two of them in action, she realized
that something about Tanner clearly spoke to Seth Mahoney, too. Because he was obviously delighted to be holding
the baby. And he seemed in no way uncomfortable performing the gesture.

Amazing. Pru couldn't think of a single man of her acquaintance who had taken such an interest in Tanner. Then
again, thanks to Tanner's presence in her life, there were
few single men of her acquaintance who had taken an interest in her, either, thereby never even meeting her son.
Well, no single men other than Dr. Mahoney, and he didn't
count. He'd take an interest in anything that had two X
chromosomes.

And now here he was, taking an interest in her son, too.
It made no sense. He was a complete womanizer, had never
made any secret of the fact that he intended to remain un-
married and unattached for the rest of his life. Yet he was
perfectly comfortable with babies, even though he assured
her he had none of his own.

Very interesting, she thought. But somehow, not particularly surprising.

Tanner began to babble incessantly then, telling Seth
Mahoney all about his hectic day before launching into

some story about heaven only knew what. And, God love him, the good doctor nodded and murmured in all the right places, eagerly encouraging the infant to continue with his story. "No," he said in feigned incredulity. "You don't say. Go on. Get outta here. I don't believe it. She said that? To *you?* And then what did you say to her?"

When Tanner finally offered Pru an entry into the conversation, she simply jutted a thumb over her shoulder and said, "I'll just go see about dinner."

"Fine," her guest told her without looking up. Then, without missing a beat, he went back to his conversation with Tanner. "Really," he said as he carried the baby toward the sofa. "Imagine that. There's just no telling what some people will do...."

With one final, bemused shake of her head, Pru turned her back on the pair and headed for the kitchen. It had been her idea that she and Seth Mahoney have dinner together tonight, so that they could talk and share information about each other and decide on their phony past as a couple.

Plus she had wanted to make sure that by the time the reunion came around Tanner would be totally comfortable with his "daddy." Although Pru figured she could foist off any shy behavior on her son's part with the excuse that he was going through some kind of baby thing, and after all, her husband worked long hours at the hospital and didn't get to spend nearly as much time with his son as he'd like to, she wanted to ease any potential tension between the two as much as she could.

Now, it appeared, she had been worried for nothing. Tanner seemed to feel perfectly at home with Dr. Mahoney. Now all Pru had to do was become as comfortable with him herself. For some reason, it seemed a rather daunting task.

Having him over for dinner a few times before their trip to Pittsburgh had seemed like a good idea. Strictly for Tan-

ner's benefit, naturally. Of course, that was before she'd
seen Dr. Mahoney in a pair of Levi's that were faded in
some *very* strategic places. That was before she had noticed
how broad his shoulders were beneath a sweater that just
begged a woman's hands to wander up beneath it. That was
before she'd seen the ease with which her son would take
to him. That was before she realized how his presence in
her home would feel.

Namely…homey. Within moments of his entering her
tiny apartment, the place already felt cozier to Pru somehow. Nicer. More welcoming. Which was saying something, because she'd made the place pretty doggone homey
already, even if she was living within a tight budget. Her
furnishings were antiques, though not of the priceless
kind—or even the expensive kind, for that matter. And
she'd accessorized them with hand-me-downs from her parents that her mother had passed along when they made the
move to Florida.

All in all, the place looked a lot like somebody's grand-
mother's apartment, all dark wood and overstuffed, flow-
ered furniture and hooked wool rugs, with touches like milk
glass and cranberry glass lamps, needlepoint pillows and
crocheted throws.

Pru liked the decor a lot and was always glad to come
home. Now, however, she wondered if she'd ever look at
her apartment quite the same way again. Suddenly, for
some reason, Seth Mahoney seemed to be a part of things
here. And the quality he added was something she wouldn't
be able to duplicate herself. Worse, it was something she
suspected—even now—that she would miss a lot, once he
was gone.

It was an odd thought, to be sure, because, in spite of
having worked with him for two years—and in spite of
having such a huge crush on him for two years—she didn't
really know him all that well. Certainly she was privy to

his charm and sense of humor, but she knew virtually nothing about his past or his life outside the hospital. She didn't know if he was a New Jersey native or if he had any siblings or where his parents lived or if he had parents at all. She knew he lived in a Cherry Hill high-rise known for its exclusive condos, and she knew he drove a late model BMW sports car. But that wasn't exactly surprising, considering the fact that he was a successful young bachelor doctor. Other than that, however, she knew nothing about him at all.

Funny, how she'd worked with him for so long without learning anything about him, Pru thought as she carried dishes into the dining room to arrange them on the table. She knew most of her co-workers in neurology pretty well, had even been to the homes of many of them. Over two years, working side by side, you usually learned a lot about someone. It was inevitable that people would reveal little snatches of their lives, however superficially. But Dr. Mahoney had never done that.

Then again, she thought further, seeing as how she'd done her best to avoid him for the entirety of his stint at Seton General, maybe her lack of knowledge about his person shouldn't come as a surprise.

When she went to announce dinner, she found Dr. Mahoney—Seth, she corrected herself, knowing she had to get used to calling him that, regardless of how strange it felt—lying on her chintz sofa. He had one arm propped behind his head, and he looked surprisingly at home on the pink and green cabbage-rose print. What was even more surprising was that he had Tanner sitting on his chest, his free hand placed resolutely at the baby's waist to keep him from falling over. But that hadn't kept Tanner from leaning down to squeeze the good doctor's nose in both fists. Dr. Mahoney—Seth, Pru corrected herself again—only chuckled at the indignity.

"Dinner is, ah…it's ready…when you are," she said, stumbling over the words because of the sight she was trying hard to absorb.

Dr. Mahoney—Seth—turned at her announcement, baby fingers still curled around his nose, looking almost as if he'd forgotten she was there. "Right," he finally replied, carefully levering himself upward. Tanner slapped both of his fat baby hands playfully against Dr. Mahoney's—Seth's—cheeks, and Dr. Mahoney—Seth—laughed harder.

"Cute kid you've got here, Prudence," he said softly as he stood.

She smiled. "Yeah, I think so, too. I've pretty much decided I'm going to keep him, even after the one-year trial period is up."

"Smart woman," Seth told her with as he hefted Tanner into his arms and crossed the living room toward her. "Did you get the extended warranty on him?"

She chuckled, then shook her head. "No, I couldn't afford it. But I think I'll keep him all the same."

"Wise move. He's a definite keeper."

She sighed wistfully, crossed her arms over her midsection in what felt like a defensive pose for some reason and spoke without thinking. "I just wish his father had felt that way."

As Seth halted in front of her, something dark and unreadable flickered in his eyes, so briefly that Pru was almost—*almost*—certain she had imagined it. "Do you?" he asked levelly.

She thought a little bit more about it, then lifted one shoulder and let it drop. "Well, maybe not. As awful as it was when Kevin left, I'm not sure he and I had something that would have lasted, regardless of Tanner's arrival. And he obviously wasn't cut out to be a father, if he couldn't even hang around for Tanner's birth. I suppose I should be relieved that I discovered that sooner, rather than later, when it would have been harder for both of us.''

Seth was silent a moment, then said, ''I suppose you should be.''

''Still,'' she continued, her gaze falling to her son, who was too fascinated by a loose thread on Seth's sweater to notice her study, ''it's going to be hard to raise him alone. If he were a girl, I don't think I'd worry so much, because I think I could be a good influence there.

''Well, reasonably good,'' she amended, recalling that irresponsible thing. ''But I feel as though little boys need to have a good masculine influence in their lives, and Tanner just doesn't have that. With my father living in Florida, I'm not sure the little guy's needs in that department are going to be met at all. And he's such a sweet kid.'' Something twisted tight inside her as she added, ''I hate to think of him growing up to become a surly, resentful adolescent, just because his mother screwed up and let him down when he was a baby.''

Unable to stand even the meager distance that separated her from her son, Pru moved forward to gently pluck him from Seth's arms, then snuggled him close, tucking his head beneath her chin. She pressed a soft kiss to his downy crown, then closed her eyes and held him closer still.

She didn't care if her behavior was irrational. She was a new mother. She was entitled. She was still trying to deal with the surge of new emotions and fears and anxieties that daily erupted inside her. Someday, she supposed, she'd reach a point where every day *didn't* hold a new crisis or a new developmental milestone—for Tanner *or* for her. Then again, maybe she wouldn't. For now, though, she was content to be irrational when it came to her child. And she didn't care if Seth Mahoney witnessed it.

Hey, she told herself. He was her husband, at least for a

while. He'd better get used to all the new-mom... stuff...that went along with parenting.

Seth watched Prudence as she closed her eyes and cradled her young son close, as if she were trying to calm herself or rid herself of some heinous fear. And as he watched, something deep inside him that he hadn't even realized was cold began to grow warm. He'd always thought she was a beautiful, desirable woman. But she'd never been much more to him than that. Now, suddenly, there was a new dimension to her character that he'd never fully considered.

For the first time, Seth was seeing that Prudence Holloway was human. Very human. And something about that triggered a response in him unlike anything he'd ever felt before. He didn't normally view people as human. Not really. Oh, sure, he knew that they had feelings and thoughts and values and opinions. And he knew that some were good and some were bad, though he was generally of the opinion that the vast majority were of the former crowd.

But he'd never really viewed people as being *human.* He'd viewed *himself* as human. And he'd never thought of others in terms of being like *him,* nor himself in terms of being like others. He'd never considered that they all shared the same essence and makeup, or that they were all members of one species. People were different from him. They always had been. Therefore, he'd always reasoned, people couldn't possibly be human.

To Seth, that made perfect sense.

Throughout his entire life, he'd never felt a real bond with anyone. He'd never felt as if he fit in anywhere. He wasn't sure why that was, only that it was true. And he'd never harbored any bitterness or anxiety about feeling different. But he had always felt alone. As if there was something about him that other people simply didn't share, or that there was something about other people that *he* simply didn't share.

For that reason he'd just always felt as if he were human where others were…something else. Nothing bad, nothing inferior, nothing less substantial than he was. Just something…else. Something different. Something he could never be himself.

With Prudence, though, he felt a strange sort of kinship. Why? He had no idea. But there was something in her that spoke to something in him. And he decided then that he'd like very much to find out what it was.

"I don't know," he said softly as he watched her nuzzle the side of Tanner's neck, watched, too, as Tanner responded by pressing his wet, open mouth to her cheek in what might just be a kiss. "Looks to me like you've done pretty well by the little guy. He doesn't seem to be suffering from any kind of lack in his life."

When she glanced up from her son to meet Seth's gaze, there was something in her eyes that confirmed his suspicion about the two of them sharing some unnameable, indecipherable…thing. And for just the briefest of moments he thought she detected the presence of that thing, too. Because for just the briefest of moments, she seemed to crawl inside Seth. And as she went, she seemed to absorb a part of him inside herself, too.

Then that instant was gone, and he was back where he had been before, standing in the arched doorway that separated Prudence Holloway's living room from her dining room. The warm, filmy sense of joining was over, and the fuzzy, heady feeling of knowledge was gone. But in that moment something was different between them. He could feel it. And when he looked at Prudence, he sensed that she felt it, too.

But, just as he had, she seemed to snap out of it, because she shook her head, almost imperceptibly, as if trying to

physically clear it of some errant idea. And then that odd
sharing between them was well and truly gone.

At least, he thought, for now.

"I'm not going to stand here and tell you that it's been
easy so far raising Tanner alone," she said, returning to
their earlier discussion. "Because it hasn't been. Raising
him by myself is the hardest thing I've ever done. But I
feel like it's probably a piece of cake right now, compared
to what's coming. I'm just not sure I'm equipped to handle
all the guy stuff that's bound to come later. I mean, how
am I supposed to explain the whole male experience to him,
when I don't know a single thing about men?"

Seth smiled, thinking she probably knew a lot more than
she realized. But all he said was, "You'll be fine, Prudence." Of that, he was absolutely certain.

She smiled back, but he could see that she didn't share
his conviction. "I wish I could be as confident as you are,"
she said softly.

"Someday you doubtless will be."

It was a cryptic statement, but he decided not to expound
upon it. The two of them were getting along surprisingly
well, and he didn't want to jeopardize the fragile bond they
were creating. Besides, he wasn't exactly sure what he'd
meant by the comment, not really. Not yet. And maybe,
deep down, he just didn't think it was a good idea to follow
this line of dialogue.

So he said, "What are we having for dinner?"

The question effectively scattered what little bits of ir-
resolution lingered, thereby releasing them both from the
spell that had descended over them. Prudence's smile this
time was a bit less curious than her last had been, and she
seemed to feel as if she were on steadier ground.

Well, Seth thought, that made one of them.

"Pasta," she told him. "It's the only thing I can make

that I never mess up. Well, almost never," she quickly amended. "It's baked ziti."

"Sounds faboo."

She chuckled. "Yeah, well, it's something Tanner can eat, too. He loves Italian. And this will be easy for him to gum."

"Gee, I can't imagine a better testimonial than that," Seth told her. "I don't know about you two, but I'm starved."

Strange, though, he thought, how food was suddenly the last thing on his mind.

Prudence tipped her head to one side, toward the table behind herself. "Shall we, then?" she asked.

Unbidden an idea exploded into his head, and it involved using that dining room table in a manner that was in no way what it had been intended for. He smiled. "By all means," he said, thinking that maybe, just maybe, he and Prudence could enjoy their dessert there later, after Tanner had gone to bed.

A man could dream, couldn't he?

Six

Seth was genuinely surprised by how much he enjoyed having dinner with Prudence Holloway and her infant son. Everything about it was just so...so nice. So warm. The casual conversation, the pleasant companionship, the tasty food, the hurling of pasta against every conceivable surface, and the customary hosing down of the infant afterward. Yes, all in all, Seth enjoyed the meal enormously, and it surprised him.

But that surprise was nothing compared to the shock he received afterward. Because the moment Prudence had finished stashing their leftovers in the refrigerator and their dishes into the dishwasher, she asked him the most indecent question he'd ever been asked in his life. What she proposed was so appalling, so unthinkable, so scandalous, it left Seth speechless.

"So, you want to help me get Tanner ready for bed?"

Just like that. As if it were a completely acceptable, totally innocuous request. Honestly. What *was* the woman thinking? As if he—*he,* Dr. Seth Mahoney, man about town—would engage in something as domestic as preparing a baby for beddie-bye.

He gazed at her mildly. "You're joking, right?"

She shook her head as she lifted the marinara-smudged little tot from his high chair. "Hey, he's your son, too," she reminded him with a smile. "Even if it's only for one weekend, you need to find out what goes into his care and feeding."

Seth chuckled. "Why? Other fathers don't. And their responsibilities last far longer than one weekend."

"Sure, other fathers do," she countered. "Most dads these days take a very active role in the rearing of their children."

Seth eyed her dubiously. "Do they?"

"Of course."

"How very odd."

She shook her head and rolled her eyes. "Oh, come on. You can't tell me this is news to you."

"Actually," he said, "I think this definitely qualifies as a late-breaking bulletin."

She sighed heavily. "Boy, it's a good thing I still have six months' worth of *Parents* magazine that I haven't read yet lying around. For once, being irresponsible has panned out."

Hmm... Seth wasn't sure he liked the direction this conversation was taking. Not that he'd much cared for the initial route, either, but still. "What do you mean?" he asked. "Why will *Parents* magazine be coming in handy?

She smiled sweetly. "You can take them home for a cram session."

He eyed her with what he hoped was mild incredulity, and not the stark-raving panic he suspected it really was. "I *beg* your pardon."

Prudence's eyes sparkled mischievously, but there was something oddly appealing about that wicked twinkle, as if the two of them were sharing a joke to which no one else was privy. And Seth kind of liked the idea of the two of them sharing something exclusively that no one else would understand. In fact, he thought, he rather liked the idea a lot.

"No need to beg," she told him. "You can thank me later. There's all kinds of information in there for you to pick up. We can go over it together next week."

He hesitated a moment as he let that sink in. Not just the part about there being a *together next week*—which sounded very promising indeed—but also the part about... Hmmm... "Are you telling me there's going to be a quiz?" he asked.

She nodded. "Next week," she repeated. "Same bat time, same bat channel. I'll fix scampi, and then we can review. So you better start studying tonight."

He eyed her narrowly. "Will there be math?"

She waggled her head back and forth a bit. "Some."

Seth eyed her more narrowly. "Will it be multiple choice?"

"Maybe."

He studied her intently for a moment, wondering how much of a game this was that they were playing. Cautiously he told her, "I'll warn you right now that I'm not good with essay questions, Prudence. I'm much better with straightforward facts. Shades of gray elude me. I've always done better seeing in black-and-white. It would be best if you made this true or false."

She didn't seem at all intimidated by his response, because she only smiled at him indulgently. Not that he was necessarily trying to intimidate her. It just seemed important for some reason that she understand where he was coming from. Of course, it might help matters if *he* understood where he was coming from, too. But that was beside the point.

"I'll remember that," she told him softly. "In the meantime, you can get a little hands-on experience helping me with Tanner tonight. If you do it right, I'll even give you extra credit."

Although that extra-credit business definitely sounded intriguing, Seth wasn't sure how much of an extra effort he wanted to put forth to achieve it. Especially if it meant getting down-and-dirty with a baby. True, he loved children, and he found babies to be particularly enchanting. However. Babies took that down and dirty stuff much too seriously, as evidenced by Tanner's gleeful distribution of ziti not long ago. And a man could only be expected to do so much for his reward.

When Seth had agreed to take part in this charade, he'd been thinking more along the lines of posing as Prudence's husband, and less—much less—along the lines of posing as Tanner's father. He had just never fully considered what all went into the care and feeding of the creatures. Sure, he liked to spend his breaks in the hospital nursery, watching the neonatal nurses there do their thing, but that was just the point. *He* was watching. *They* were doing.

The closest *he* ever came to actually participating was to occasionally pluck one of the newborns gently out of his or her bassinet, and sit in a nearby rocking chair for a moment, holding the squirming little bundle. If he was feeling particularly sentimental, he might even hum a few bars of "Heartbreak Hotel" to soothe the baby to sleep. But that was as far as he'd been willing to go in his close encounters of the infant kind.

It was the dilemma that plagued Seth's life: his desire—almost a need—to have a family and his unwillingness to experience firsthand everything that such a condition involved. And not just where the children thing was concerned, either, he realized. But where the wife thing was concerned, as well.

When Seth dreamed of his future, it was always in a vague, rosy, indistinct sort of way. The way he envisioned it, he had his work, of course, and a big house to go home to in the evenings when the workday was through. There was a faceless, though beautiful, woman to greet him at the door with a martini, and a handful of handsome—and equally faceless—children romping at his feet. He kissed them all in turn, then headed for the living room to unwind while they all told him—in total harmony, of course— about their respective days.

He supposed that the reason he wanted his future to resemble that scene was because his past was in no way similar. Growing up penniless without a father, and with a mother who was at work more than she as at home, Seth supposed he shouldn't be surprised by his desire to create some retro Beaver Cleaver sort of existence for himself.

Still, he wished he hadn't turned out to be so damnably predictable, so nauseatingly sentimental. Because suddenly that faceless wife in his fantasy was taking on the identity of Prudence Holloway. And suddenly those faceless children were beginning to resemble Tanner. Here in the Holloway home, Seth was beginning to see that—

God help him. He was beginning to think that maybe, just maybe, his imaginary future had the potential to be every bit as real—and every bit as wonderful—as he had conceived it. And with the realization that his dreams might very well someday come true, Seth found that he was absolutely terrified.

Prudence seemed to sense his misgivings, because she patted him on the arm with much reassurance. Oh, yes. That was certainly the response he had been hoping to rouse in her this evening. A pat of reassurance. Well, my, my, my.

Wasn't their relationship just progressing by leaps and bounds now.

"Don't worry," she told him. "Tonight you can just watch and take notes. We won't worry about the lab technique until next week, 'kay?"

It took him a moment to remember that they had been discussing the baby's bedtime preparation. But even at that, it wasn't Seth's lab technique that he found himself worrying about. No, it was an entirely different technique that suddenly had him concerned.

Because on the heels of his epiphany about his future came yet another epiphany. Prudence, was standing in her kitchen—her *kitchen,* without question the *least* sexy room in a home. And she was covered with marinara that her child—her *child*—had tossed lovingly upon her. And she was dressed in a baggy—*baggy*—turtleneck sweater—*turtleneck sweater.* And she had just informed him that they were going to prepare a baby—a *baby*—for bed.

Normally any one of these developments on a date would have Seth scrambling for an excuse to put an end to the evening, as quickly and painlessly as possible. Yet here was a woman who was guilty of perpetrating a half dozen crimes of nonpassion, and he was getting aroused. Because all he could do was stand there thinking that once that baby of hers was in his bed, then he and the woman in question should certainly retire to hers.

It made no sense. There was absolutely nothing about this moment—about this entire night—that had been sexually arousing. Yet Seth had been sexually aroused virtually from the moment he'd entered the apartment. And the sight of Prudence all rumpled and stained in her kitchen made something inside him go whirring out of control.

He knew he should put an end to the evening, as quickly and painlessly as possible. In fact, he knew it would be best if he just backed out of this whole Mr. Prudence Holloway

charade before things went any further. He was crazy to
have agreed to go along in the first place, even if he was
essentially the one responsible for putting Prudence in her
current situation. There was only so much a man could do,
after all, to aid a damsel in distress. Even if he was the one
who had caused that distress.

Seth told himself to say something—anything—to escape
the remainder of the evening. That he had to go home. That
he had an early surgery scheduled in the morning. That he
just remembered an important long-distance phone call he
had to make. That he was terrified of the domestic scene
laid out before him, and he had to run screaming in horror
in the other direction, so if Prudence could just excuse him
now, he'd be on his merry way.

But what he heard coming out of his mouth, dammit,
was, "Okay. I'd love to help put Tanner to bed."

Pru told herself she should have ended this evening a
looooong time ago, before things had gone too far. A good
time might have been when she'd glanced up from her dinner plate to find Seth gazing at her as if he wanted to make
her dessert. Or maybe even further back, she amended.
Back when she'd seen him lying on the couch with Tanner
sitting on his chest. Or maybe even further back still. Like
when she'd opened the front door and felt her stomach drop
to her toes, because she'd wanted to welcome him to her
home in a manner that was far too intimate for a simple
salutation.

At any rate, she should have done it long before now.
Because now she was beginning to think it would be impossible to tell Seth to leave. Not just because Tanner was
reluctant to release him, but because Prudence herself
didn't want to let him go.

As she stood framed in her son's doorway, watching
Seth, who was enthroned in the rocking chair with Tanner

PLAY

RUN
FOR THE
ROSES

and get
THREE FREE GIFTS!

HOW TO PLAY:

1. With a coin, carefully scratch off the silver box at the right. Then check the claim chart to see what we have for you — **2 FREE BOOKS** and a **FREE GIFT**—**ALL YOURS FREE!**

2. Send back the card and you'll receive two brand-new Silhouette Desire® novels. These books have a cover price of $3.99 each in the U.S. and $4.50 each in Canada, but they are yours to keep absolutely free.

3. There's no catch. You're under no obligation to buy anything. We charge nothing — ZERO — for your first shipment. And you don't have to make any minimum number of purchases — not even one!

4. The fact is, thousands of readers enjoy receiving books by mail from the Silhouette Reader Service™. They enjoy the convenience of home delivery...they like getting the be new novels at discount prices, BEFORE they're available in stores... and they love their *Heart to Heart* subscriber newsletter featuring author news, horoscopes, recipes, book reviews and much more!

5. We hope that after receiving your free books you'll want to remain a subscriber. But the choice is yours — to continue or cancel, any time at all! So why not take us up on our invitation, with no risk of any kind. You'll be glad you did!

Visit us online at
www.eHarlequin.com

in his lap, reading *Pat the Bunny,* something deep inside her seemed to be growing larger. At first she had no idea what that something was. Then, gradually, it dawned on her, much to her distress, that what was slowly expanding inside her was her affection for Seth Mahoney.

Affection. For Seth Mahoney. Honestly, as if she didn't have enough complications in her life right now.

She had been hoping that she'd just been imagining that for the past two years. She had been hoping that she was mistaken about the warm, fuzzy feelings that came over her whenever he was around. She had been hoping those were just the result of some strange hormonal reaction or maybe some odd, heretofore undiscovered chemistry or perhaps some of those endorphins she read so much about. She hadn't thought she might genuinely care for him.

Now, however, she was beginning to think otherwise.

Ever since Seth Mahoney's arrival at Seton General—even during those months when Pru had been involved with someone else—she had been fascinated, charmed and unwillingly captivated by Dr. Irresistible. There was no point in denying it any longer, she told herself. She liked Seth Mahoney. She had liked him for some time. And now that she had forced herself to admit that, she would have to be careful and guard that affection. She would have to make sure that it never turned into anything more substantial.

Unfortunately, that growing feeling inside her was a pretty good indication that she wasn't going to be able to keep it under wraps much longer. Because as she watched Seth get to the part in the book about ''Daddy's scratchy face,'' as she noted the smile that curled his lips when Tanner laughed and slapped a hand against his rough cheeks, the affection inside Pru turned into something else entirely.

She just couldn't let herself think about what that *something else* might be.

Pushing the troubling thoughts away, she concentrated instead on Tanner, marveling at the ease with which he had accepted Seth. Boy, you think you know your kid, then *boom*. He totally surprises you. Pru wasn't sure she'd ever stop being amazed by her son.

"Okay, buckaroo, that's the end of that," Seth said, closing the book and setting it on the dresser beside the rocking chair. He tucked his hands under Tanner's armpits and drew the baby up to standing in his lap. "Now I think it's time for your mommy to get you settled into bed."

Taking her cue, Pru covered the handful of steps necessary to bring her into Tanner's room. She had quickly changed her clothes while Seth read *Jamberry* to her son, not just because of the marinara accessories she had donned during dinner, but also because of the numerous water spots that had come about during Tanner's bath. Now she wore a pair of blue jeans and cropped red sweater, both dry and clean.

In her haste, she hadn't thought much about the outfit—it had just been lying in the chair by her bed and was most convenient. But when she saw the heat that lit Seth's eyes when his gaze fell upon her, she wondered if maybe she should have stayed with being damp and tomatoey. Damp and tomatoey was in no way conducive to dangerous glances. This outfit, however, evidently was. Because his gaze kept settling on the swell of her hips, kept homing in on what she belatedly realized must be a hint of skin revealed between the waistband of her jeans and the hem of her sweater.

She tugged self-consciously at the latter garment, knowing the gesture would be futile. Sure enough, when she released it, her sweater popped right back up again, drawing even more attention to the flesh beneath. She knew that, because Seth's pupils expanded wildly, nearly eclipsing the blue of his irises.

"Uh," she began eloquently, "I'll just, um…I'll, uh…I'll take it from here," she finally got out. "It should only take a few minutes. He's had a busy day, and for the past month or two, he's been a really good sleeper. Lately he's been sleeping like…well, like a baby." She felt herself on the verge of babbling incoherently, so she jutted a thumb nervously over her shoulder. "If you want to pour some more wine…?"

She let her voice trail off, not so much because she figured Seth knew what she meant, but because the flicker of heat in his eyes suddenly became a raging, volcanic rush.

"I'll be glad to," he said softly.

To her surprise, before he handed Tanner over to her care, he placed a quick kiss at the baby's crown. It was a sweet, touching gesture, one that nurtured the growing affection inside Pru. As if that needed tending, she thought. As if it wasn't already growing wildly out of control all by itself.

After relinquishing the baby, Seth brushed his thumb one final time over Tanner's cheek, a gesture that brought him a soft coo of delight in response. For a moment Pru wasn't sure if it had been she or Tanner who uttered that coo, but when Seth smiled at the baby, she realized it must have been her son. Something about his smile, though, twisted her stomach into a knot. He looked like a man who desperately wanted something he knew he would never—could never—have. And she found herself wanting to give it to him with all her heart, if only she could figure out what it was.

Before she had a chance to ask him, he turned his gaze to her, and she was rendered silent by the profound melancholy she saw reflected in his eyes. "I'll see you in a few minutes," he said quietly.

And all Pru could do was nod and watch him go.

* * *

Once he was free of Tanner's sanctuary, Seth actually did a good bit more than pour wine. He turned off all but one light, a standing lamp in the corner that left the room bathed in a pale, milky glow. Then he switched on Prudence's sound system, lowering the volume to the "a little romance" setting. Then he made a thorough inspection of her sparse assortment of CDs, grimacing at the eclectic collection of heavy metal and seventies bubblegum pop—what *had* her parents been thinking?—until he located something that suited his mood. *Gershwin for Lovers,* it said on the case. Perfect.

By the time she rejoined him—which, as she'd promised, wasn't long—he was all set. Glass in hand, he had tucked himself into the corner of the sofa, and he was humming along to "He Loves, She Loves." When Prudence entered, he lifted his wine to her in silent salute, then nodded his head toward the other glass, sitting atop the steamer trunk that served as her coffee table.

And then, very, very softly, he said, "Join me."

Just two little words, but, oh, what a wealth of implication behind them. At least, Seth hoped there was a wealth of implication behind them. Because there were so many things he wanted to imply where Prudence Holloway was concerned.

Evidently, he succeeded, because in response to his request, she turned as white as a sheet and swallowed visibly. Then her eyes widened to the size of silver dollars, and she stammered "I...I...I..."

He fought off a smile.

"I...I...I...okay," she agreed.

This time he fought off a chuckle.

She tugged anxiously, ineffectually, at her sweater again, and, much to Seth's delight, it bounced back up as it had before. Her jeans were loose-fitting enough that the waistband had dipped a bit below her navel, and he found himself thinking, as he had in Tanner's room a few moments ago, what an adorable navel it was. And suddenly he found himself making all kinds of plans where that navel was concerned. Her jeans *weren't* so loose, however, that he couldn't make out the elegant flair of her hips, or the trim thighs beneath the softly faded fabric. And my, but he found himself making plans for those hips and thighs, too.

Goodness, but the evening was starting to look up.

With obvious trepidation Prudence scooped the glass of wine up from the steamer trunk, then started to move toward an overstuffed club chair that was, in Seth's opinion, much too far away.

"Ah, ah, ah," he said. When she hesitated and turned back around, he smiled and flattened his palm against the sofa cushion beside him. Then he patted it gently several times, his meaning, he hoped, quite clear.

Again Prudence swallowed hard, and she seemed to be giving much consideration to her dilemma. Because she neither moved closer to the couch, nor did she seat herself in the chair. She only stood midway between, as if pondering the situation with much deliberation, trying to decide which position held more danger.

Silly girl, Seth thought. If she sat down in that chair, it would only provoke him.

As if she'd read his thoughts, Prudence made a quick decision and completed the three steps necessary to put her in front of the sofa. But instead of sitting in the middle, next to Seth, she placed herself at the opposite end, crowding her body against the armrest as much as she possibly could.

Seth sighed. Did she honestly think that was going to stop him?

"So," he began, scooting himself down the length of the sofa until scarcely an inch separated them. He draped an arm along the back, bending his elbow until he could hook his free hand over her shoulder. But he didn't—quite—touch her, something that seemed to make her inordinately nervous. Hoping to provoke that nervousness even more—goodness, but he was having fun—he dipped his head until scarcely a breath of air separated his mouth from her ear. Then very, very softly he whispered, "Tell me about this 'most irresponsible' business."

He wasn't sure if she was relieved or vexed by the subject he'd introduced. "Oh...you don't want to...to hear about that," she said softly, and, if he wasn't mistaken—and he rarely was—a bit breathlessly, too.

"Oh...yes, I do," he assured her, inching his body nearer still.

"Seth..." she said, the warning in her voice unmistakable.

He smiled at the sound of his name falling from her lips, even if it was a bit lacking in the warmth—nay, the *heat*—he'd hoped to someday hear attached to it. "I like the way you say my name," he told her, leaning back a bit—but not too much.

"Seth..." she repeated. The warning this time was edged with menace.

"Hmmm?" he said, moving closer once again. He thought it best to keep her guessing about his motives at this point. Mainly because he had no idea himself what he was going to do next.

The scent of her perfume was taunting him, a mixture of something sweet and spicy that he wanted to bury his nose in. So he lowered his head to the elegant curve where her neck joined her shoulder and deftly nuzzled the warm, fragrant skin he found there. Oh...how lovely the sensation was....

Prudence seemed to think so, too, because when he brushed his lips lightly over her collarbone, she uttered a soft sound of what he hoped very much was surrender. Unfortunately, what she said quickly dispelled that idea.

"This isn't what we're supposed to be doing," she told him.

However, there wasn't an ounce of conviction in her tone. And in spite of her assurance, she tilted her head fractionally to the side in a way that suggested the action was simply instinctive and in no way planned. It was an action that facilitated Seth's efforts quite nicely. And there was no way he was going to *not* take advantage.

"Isn't it?" he asked, turning his own head to move his mouth against the slender column of her throat. Over and over he brushed his lips lightly along her warm, fragrant flesh. And with every feather-like stroke of his mouth, he felt himself growing harder, more rigid, both inside and out.

"No, it's not," she whispered almost silently. But she didn't pull away.

Seth parted his lips and now dragged his open mouth more insistently up and down the side of her neck, reveling at the ripple of frantic breath that escaped her when he did. "Then what are we supposed to be doing, Prudence?" He posed the quiet question against her damp skin.

She swallowed, and he kissed each of the muscles of her throat as they worked over it. "Oh…" she moaned softly. Then, evidently remembering their dubious conversation, she said, "We-we're supposed to be getting to know each other better."

He chuckled low, then lifted his hand to curl his fingers around her nape. "Well, if you'll just give me a few more minutes," he murmured, "I promise you that we will be *intimately* acquainted."

Seven

Prudence leaped up from the couch just as he was going in for the full pounce, something that left him clutching an armful of air. He glanced up to find her standing in the middle of the room, one hand held palm out in the internationally recognized gesture of "Back off," the fingers of her other hand clutched so tightly around the bowl of her wineglass he feared she would shatter it. Placing his own glass on the steamer trunk, he stood and took a small step toward her. In response, she immediately took one giant step backward, in retreat.

Seth stopped where he was, hooking his hands loosely on his hips. "Prudence, I'm not going to hurt you. And I'm not going to try and make you do something you don't want to do."

She said nothing in response to that, only stood her ground, her dark brows furrowed.

He sighed heavily. "I just thought that tonight was supposed to be a chance for us to, as you said, get to know each other better.''

She eyed him warily, then conceded, ''It *is* supposed to be that.''

Seth tried again. ''Then why aren't we…you know… getting to know each other better?''

''You and I obviously have different opinions about what exactly 'getting to know each other better' means. That—'' she pointed at the spot on the couch they had just vacated, but he noticed she didn't look at it ''—wasn't the kind of…of…of *knowing* I had in mind.''

He held her gaze for a long, meaningful moment, arching one brow in silent query. Then, just in case she didn't understand—which he sincerely doubted—he put voice to that query. ''Wasn't it?''

A hot stain of red crept into her cheeks, and he knew that whatever she was about to say would be a big fat lie. ''Of course it wasn't.''

Yep. A big fat lie, for sure.

''Look, Prudence,'' he said trying again, ''if we're supposed to be married—with child, no less—then we're going to have to get comfortable being physical with each other. As long as we have Tanner with us, people are going to know that we've…you know…at least once.''

''We have *not*…you know…*even* once,'' she quickly pointed out.

''Well, nowhere but in our hearts and minds,'' he said, smiling.

She shook her head. ''I've *never*—''

''Oh, you have, too,'' he interrupted her before she embarrassed herself. ''Don't even try to deny it.''

Surprisingly, she didn't. She only clamped her lips shut tight, as if she were afraid they might spring open again to reveal something she'd rather not have revealed.

So Seth continued. ''We've—you know—many, *many*

times in *my* heart and *my* mind. And trust me, Prudence, it's always been very, *very* good. But then, I suspect you know that already. Because I suspect we've done it more than a few times in your heart and your mind, too.''

She eyed him in silence for a moment, and he wondered if she was going to try to offer up another big fat lie. What she did, however, was sidestep the comment completely. Damn her.

''That's not why you were getting physical with me,'' she said. ''It had nothing to do with the…the image…you think we should present at my high school reunion.''

Well, duh, he thought. ''No, Prudence, you're absolutely right—that wasn't why I was getting physical with you.''

She seemed surprised that he would admit such a thing flat-out the way he had. Somehow, Seth refrained from rolling his eyes. ''The reason I was getting physical with you is because I've spent nearly every single night of my life since meeting you wondering what it would be like to make love to you.''

She exhaled a little gasp of disbelief, even though Seth was certain there was no way she could possibly find unbelievable such a revelation. Hadn't he gone out of his way to make clear his desire for her? Hadn't he stopped just short of begging? Then again, he *hadn't* stopped short of begging, he recalled now. So how could his assertion possibly come as news to her?

He took an experimental step forward, and when she didn't flee in terror, he continued. ''The reason I was getting physical with you,'' he said softly as he approached her, ''was because it's something that's been coming, something that's been building, for two years. *Two years,* Prudence.''

This time there was no gasp of disbelief in response, only a small gape of confusion. Or, perhaps, indecision. Something inside Seth fluttered hopefully at the realization.

He braved yet another step toward her and went on. "The reason I was getting physical with you is because I know it's something you've been wondering about yourself—what it would be like between the two of us."

Her mouth closed at that, forming neither confirmation nor denial of his charge. No matter, Seth thought. He already knew the answer. She wanted him. He was—almost—sure of it.

Another step forward brought him within touching range of her. And although touching her was precisely what he wanted to do, something in her eyes prevented him from acting on his impulse—just yet. "And the reason I was getting physical with you is because…"

He sighed his defeat, extending a hand halfheartedly toward her, as if by doing so he might be able to pull the right words out of thin air. But, much to his own disbelief, what emerged from his mouth when he began to speak again was the truth.

"Because frankly, Prudence, I…I can't resist you."

And with that, he finally gave in to two years of wanting her, succumbing to the desire—to the absolute need—to have Prudence in his arms in the way he had always imagined having her. Willing. Needful. Passionate. Hungry.

And when he lifted the glass from her hand and set it on the steamer trunk next to his own, when he pulled her into his embrace and covered her mouth with his, that was exactly the way she responded. Willingly. Needfully. Passionately. Hungrily.

After one single, solitary, oh-so-soft sound of indecision, her lips beneath his parted eagerly in welcome, and she wound her arms around his back as if that was exactly where they belonged. Seth tangled his fingers in her hair and tilted her head backward a bit, then he tasted her as deeply as he could. And when Prudence boldly tucked her hands up under his sweater and splayed them open over

the bare skin of his back, they both groaned aloud their
need for each other, and their relief at finally—*finally*—
coming together this way.

Taking her cue, Seth, too, dropped a hand to dip it under
the hem of her sweater, inching his fingers slowly upward
over the hot, satiny skin he encountered beneath. He danced
them leisurely along her rib cage, his fingertips sliding intimately over each elegant bone as they climbed higher…
and higher…and higher still. His thumb curved around to
her front as his fingers opened more intimately over her
back, until he deftly cradled the lower curve of her breast
in the *L* shape created between thumb and forefinger. Prudence emitted a long low sound of arousal at the contact,
and Seth replied with an equally needful groan of his own.

Unable to help himself, he nudged his hand upward, cupping his palm fully over the soft mound of her breast. He
felt her nipple pushing against the lace of her brassiere, and
he rubbed the pad of his thumb back and forth over the
rigid little bud. She gasped again and pulled her mouth
from his, and he hesitated before going any further. But
instead of retreating from him, as he had feared she would,
she nuzzled her nose and mouth against his throat, trailing
the tip of her tongue along his Adam's apple.

Sweet. Ah, she felt so sweet. Seth's blood roared in his
ears at the delicate contact, and he fought the threat as his
knees began to buckle. His eyes fluttered closed at the damp
path her tongue was taking, and he seized full possession
of her breast. Flattening his palm over the plump globe, he
rolled it in gentle circles before closing his fingers more
intimately over her again.

When he did, he nearly chuckled with delight at his discovery—his thumb connected with a front hook closure on
her brassiere. Without hesitation, without plan, without

thought, Seth deftly flicked it open, then scooped the wisp of lace away and filled his hand with her naked flesh.

At the moment of contact he felt one of her hands lift from his back, and he started to protest her withdrawal. But before he could adequately form the words—hell, before he could adequately form the *thought*—he felt her hand elsewhere, in a much more intriguing place than it had been before.

Prudence ran her fingers up and down along his thigh, pressing them intimately against the taut muscles until he felt his flesh coming alive. Then she began to draw circles, exquisitely erotic circles, each one slightly larger in circumference than the one before. As he stroked and palmed her breast, slowly, slowly, oh...so slowly, those circles expanded, until they spanned from the bottom curve of his buttock to the fly of his jeans.

"Yes," he murmured, uncertain when he'd elected to speak, uncertain even what question he had answered with that single, roughly uttered, word.

Prudence seemed to know, though, because after only a slight hesitation, she hooked her fingers beneath the waistband of his jeans. Seth sucked in a breath as she flicked open the first button of his fly. Then he held that breath as she moved down to the next. And then the next. And then the two more following that. But she faltered before going any farther, even as his hardening flesh surged up against the faded denim to greet her touch.

For some reason he was reluctant to encourage any further exploration on her part, even though he was impatient to feel the glide of her fingers along his stiff shaft. She needed to move at her own pace, he thought, just as he needed to move at his. His own pace, however, was significantly faster than hers was, because he faltered not at all as he scooted her sweater high above her breasts.

For a moment he only stood gazing at her, marveling at

the soft, pink perfection he held in his hand. In that moment
he realized he had never wanted anything in his life more
than he wanted to have Prudence Holloway in his mouth.
His utter and inescapable need must have been clear, and
she must have felt the same way. Because as he lowered
his head to claim his prize, he felt her fingers creeping
along his waistband again.

As he drew her nipple full into his mouth, he felt her
fingers push past the worn denim, past, too, the soft cotton
of his briefs. And as he laved the taut, tasty peak of her
breast for the first time, he felt her fingers close around the
head of his turgid shaft. The dual sensations of utter pleasure rocked him, made him suck fiercely and pull more of
her into his mouth than he had intended. When he did, she
responded by closing her hand convulsively over him. And
Seth knew then that there would be no turning back. Not
tonight. Maybe not ever.

Oh, she tasted so delicious, so intoxicating, as he dragged
his tongue over her warm flesh again and again. And she
felt so lush, so womanly, as he cupped her blossoming
breast possessively in his hand. And she sounded so erotic,
so wanton, murmuring her pleasure as she ran her fingers
up and down the long, hard length of him. And she smelled
so seductive, so heady, in her musky response to their actions.

And Seth wanted her more than he had ever wanted a
woman in his life, down to the marrow, down to the blood,
down to the very darkness of his soul.

The totality of his response shook him profoundly.
Never—never—had he felt such a hunger for a woman.
Never—never—had he needed one this badly. But instead
of acting on that need, once he realized the immeasurable
depth of it, he jerked his entire body away. When he did,
Prudence cried out her objection with an almost feral sound
of disappointment.

And it was with no small effort that Seth kept himself from echoing the sentiment in much the same way.

It took a few moments for Prudence to understand what had happened, for her to remember where she was, what she was, who she was. And even when she finally recalled all those things, it took a few moments more for her to remember what had led up to this sudden chill that seemed to have overtaken her entire body. When realization finally dawned—dawned like a wooden stake through the heart— she couldn't believe what she had done. What *they* had done. How Seth had made her feel. Where the two of them might have ended up if he hadn't put a stop to things when he had.

The reminder that it had been he, and not she, who had finally put on the brakes troubled Prudence even more than what had happened. Somehow she knew that if he hadn't halted things where he had, then it would have only been a matter of minutes before they had found their way to her bedroom. Before they had removed what was left of their clothing. Before he had buried himself deep inside her.

Before she could stop it, a graphic depiction of that very image flashed inside her brain, of the two of them sweaty and naked in her bed, Pru bucking her hips against Seth's as he drove himself into her body again and again. Immediately she squeezed her eyes shut tight, hoping to dispel the explicit vision, but it only grew more vivid instead.

So she snapped her eyes open, to a sight even more distressing. Seth Mahoney had turned his back on her, had dropped his hands loosely to his hips, and was trying— without much success—to curb his rapid, uneven breathing. His body was completely still, save the rough rise and fall of his shoulders as he tried to restore his respiration to normal. His head was bowed, as if he were ashamed of himself, and she knew he was probably feeling pretty much the same way she felt at the moment.

Confused. Surprised. Terrified.

''Seth?'' she called out softly. But she said nothing more, mainly because she had no idea what to say.

He didn't respond, save a brief rigidity that seemed to overtake his entire body. Then he caught his breath in one long, ragged inhalation and held it. For a moment she feared he would hold it until he passed out, so still did he become. But finally he released it again in a leisurely, much more controlled manner. His back remained ramrod stiff, however, and he maintained his steadfast silence.

Not sure what compelled her to do it, Prudence took a few steps forward, halting when she had just enough room to reach out to him. She settled her fingers gingerly on his shoulder, but he spun quickly around and took a step backward, as if he couldn't tolerate even that small touch from her. So she dropped her hand back to her side and studied him closely, hoping they might salvage something of the episode, something that wouldn't jeopardize the tenuous friendship that they had begun.

His eyes were cool and distant, but she still sensed a fire burning within him that wouldn't be quenched for some time. The heat seemed to be emanating from him somehow, reaching out to wrap itself around her, inviting her to join him. His gaze fastened on hers, he reached matter-of-factly down to refasten the buttons of his fly—no easy feat considering the state of his continued, and unmistakable, arousal.

When she noted it, it was Pru's turn to spin around and turn her back on him. She felt flustered and embarrassed, and could scarcely believe she was responsible for causing such a profoundly masculine reaction. She could scarcely believe that she had cradled that part of him so intimately in her hand. And she could scarcely believe that she had been thinking about doing so much more to him, so much more with him.

And then she remembered what he had done to her, the way he had touched her, tasted her, the way he had made her feel. And the heat simmering inside her bubbled higher, carrying her nearly over the edge.

Somehow, even with trembling fingers, she managed to rearrange and refasten her bra. How could she have let this happen? She wished she could blame the wine, but she was stone-cold sober. She wished she could write it off as a result of exhaustion, but she'd been sleeping surprisingly well for the past couple of weeks. She wished she could put it down to loneliness, but she'd been lonely for a long time now, and no other man had made her throw caution to the wind the way Seth Mahoney had. She wished she could excuse it as just one of those things, but she wasn't the kind of woman to indulge in an idle fling.

Prudence even found herself wanting to blame it on being so irresponsible. But she couldn't even bring herself to do that. Because deep down she feared it wasn't irresponsibility that had made her respond to Seth the way she had. Deep down she feared it was something else entirely. She just couldn't quite bring herself to put a label on it.

She couldn't quite bring herself to call it love.

No. She was *not* in love with him. No way. He wasn't the kind of man a woman fell in love with. Even a woman who was totally irresponsible would know better than to lose herself to Seth Mahoney. He took pride in being single, made the most of his bachelorhood by keeping company with as many women as he possibly could. She was just one more conquest to him, regardless of his reasons for being here. Pru may have done some stupid, irresponsible things in her life, but falling in love with Seth Mahoney would *not* be one of them.

''Prudence?''

Unfortunately, the way her heart rumbled and purred when he said her name told her she was only kidding herself. She shoved the thought aside, crossed her arms defensively over her torso but couldn't make herself turn around. "What?" she replied softly.

For a moment he said nothing, then she heard the soft *swoosh swoosh swoosh* of his shoes over the rug as he covered the scant distance between them. When he dropped his hand to her shoulder, Prudence couldn't bring herself to shrug it off. Nor could she jerk away from him as he had her. All she could do was melt a little beneath his touch, wish that things between them were different, and pray that she regained her sanity soon.

"I, uh…I guess I should apologize," he said.

She lifted her shoulder in a faint shrug, but instead of releasing her, as she had halfway expected him to, he only curled his fingers more intimately over her. "It was just as much my fault as it was yours," she told him.

"Not really."

She glanced over her shoulder at him, but found it too difficult to meet his gaze. "Why do you say that?"

He sighed heavily, a single, joyless chuckle punctuating the sound. "Because I had a specific plan in mind when I came over here tonight," he told her. "And believe it or not, it didn't involve what just happened."

She smiled a bit sadly. "No, I imagine that by now you'd planned to be in my bed, basking in some kind of postcoital euphoria."

This time when he chuckled, it sounded almost genuine. "Well, it wouldn't necessarily have been your bed, you know. There are other pieces of furniture we could try. The dining room table, for example, can be very accommodating in a pinch."

She swallowed hard, wishing she could see the humor in his vast store of knowledge where making love was concerned. Unfortunately, the realization that he was so well versed only troubled her more. "I guess you'd know," she said softly.

He didn't comment one way or another. Instead, when she lifted her gaze to his face, he was—almost—smiling. "But even as pleasant as all that sounds," he continued, "I hadn't planned on that, either. I honestly hadn't intended for us to…"

"What?" she asked when he didn't finish the statement.

He sighed heavily again. "I didn't intend for us to go quite as far as we did," he replied quietly, and somehow she knew he was telling the truth. "Not yet, anyway," he then qualified.

She did finally turn around at that, rousing the courage to face him fully. His eyes were no longer playful and bright, but hooded and dark, offering absolutely no clue as to what he might be thinking or feeling.

"Not yet?" she echoed.

The hand that had been on her shoulder rose to her hair now, and he idly wound a dark-auburn curl around and around his forefinger. Pru let him do it, mostly because it felt nice. And because, despite the turbulence of his earlier withdrawal—or, perhaps, because of it—she felt the need for some kind of gentle, nonthreatening, physical contact.

He shook his head slowly, but his gaze was focused on the length of hair he was twining around his finger. "No, according to my game plan, we weren't supposed to get naked—or even half-naked for that matter—until at least our third date."

She narrowed her eyes at him, not sure now if he was joking or not. "Is that so?"

"It's so."

"You have it all worked out, have you?"

"Well, I thought I did." His gaze dropped to link with hers. "Obviously, I misjudged a bit."

"Obviously, you did."

His eyes—so blue, so clear, so utterly breathtaking—held her captivated. "Then again, you're turning out to be a bundle of surprises, aren't you, Prudence?"

She wanted to look away, but found that she simply could not. "What's that supposed to mean?"

He hesitated only a moment before telling her, "Nothing more than what I said."

"I don't understand."

"Neither do I."

"Seth—"

But before she could voice an objection, he was striding past her, toward the steamer trunk where their wine sat neglected. He took a glass in each hand, lifting his to his lips as he extended Pru's toward her. Reluctantly she moved forward and accepted it from him, repeating his gesture. The dark-ruby merlot tasted strong and fortifying, just what she needed to chase away the lingering confusion about what had just happened between them.

Seth seemed to think so, too, because the moment he swallowed, he filled his mouth again, savoring the taste before running the tip of his tongue along his lower lip. Pru tried not to notice.

Hah. Fat chance.

"Can we start over?" he asked suddenly. "Forget about the past few minutes and try this getting-to-know-you business again?"

She hesitated for a moment. "I don't know. Look where we ended up last time we tried it."

"Yes, well, this time we'll know the danger signs to look for, won't we?"

"I don't know," she said honestly. "Will we?"

He smiled. "I think I'll remember one or two. They'll doubtless keep me awake tonight."

Pru enjoyed another—very large—swallow of wine and

decided not to press her luck. "Okay. We can start over. But you sit over there—" she pointed to the couch "—and I'll sit over there." She pointed to the overstuffed club chair.

He smiled devilishly. "Still don't trust me, do you, Prudence?"

She smiled back, letting him think whatever he wanted. The truth was, she didn't trust herself. But there was no reason he had to know that.

"Fine," he told her as he settled himself on the couch as she had instructed him. "Then maybe we should just start off with the basics and vital statistics. Where you grew up, where you went to college, where your family is now, number of siblings, birthday, favorite color, that kind of thing."

Pru, too, moved toward the chair she had opted to use herself, but even putting significant physical distance between them couldn't quite soothe her troubled soul. "That's a lot to cover in one night," she told him.

He waited until she was gazing at him full on, then said, "Not when you consider the alternative."

Oops. Oh, yeah. "Fine," she said. "Then make yourself comfortable. We could be here for a while."

Eight

It didn't occur to Pru until the following week that, although she had spilled her guts to Seth that ill-fated night in her apartment, she still knew absolutely nothing of importance about him.

Oh, sure, he had filled her in on the superficial details—how he'd graduated from high school at sixteen, how he had breezed through medical school on a full academic scholarship and had completed his residency without any major setbacks. She'd learned that he was born in New Hampshire, that he was an only child and that both of his parents had passed away some time ago. She knew that his birthday was August thirteenth, that his favorite color was blue and that his favorite author was Bernard Cornwell.

But she knew nothing of his childhood adventures, nothing of what his dreams and hopes for the future were, nothing of what he considered most important in life. He'd easily sidestepped all those questions, deeming them insignificant and boring and totally unnecessary for what the two of them had planned.

At the time Pru hadn't pressed, had figured that maybe he was right, that there really wasn't much chance such philosophical topics would arise in conversation at a high school reunion. What the two of them needed to focus on was getting their stories straight about their own bogus relationship—how and where they had met and married, particulars about Tanner's birth and early weeks, details about their current phony lifestyle. So they had spent the bulk of that first date—and a few that had followed during the past week—building that house of cards.

And it was, in fact, a house of cards they were building. Pru knew that because with each new level they constructed, the sick feeling in the pit of her stomach grew worse. In spite of that, construction had continued and was slowly nearing completion.

Seth had friends who owned a big house in Cherry Hill, a house he'd photographed extensively last summer when he'd attended a Fourth of July party there. It was this house, they'd decided, that they would adopt as their alleged residence. As for their alleged relationship, they'd thought it might be best to stick to the facts as much as possible. They had become acquainted when Seth had come to work at Seton General. Sparks had flown immediately. That much, at least, Pru took comfort in realizing, was true. Within six months of meeting, they impulsively ran off to Atlantic City to marry. They had conceived Tanner on their honeymoon.

In two weeks, when it came time to attend the reunion, they planned to rent a top-of-the-line sport utility vehicle to make the three-hour drive to Pittsburgh. They had concluded that Pru's ten-year-old Toyota sedan wasn't classy enough, and Seth's BMW roadster wasn't big enough, to pass muster for the kind of upper-middle-class family they were pretending to be.

He had brought over his luggage the last time he'd come to the apartment, because the patched and mismatched duffel bags Pru normally took on trips might raise eyebrows. She'd already started sorting through her wardrobe, to pick out the best pieces, items she hadn't worn since before Tanner's birth, either because they hadn't fit until recently, or because she hadn't wanted to risk their becoming soiled with baby food and baby byproducts.

She couldn't believe the depth of the deception she was about to perpetrate. Nothing in her current lifestyle was appropriate for the charade they were about to perform. Had she realized how extensive the lie was going to have to be, she would have corrected it long ago.

You still have time, a little voice piped up from inside. *You don't have to go through with this. You can back out anytime. It would be the* responsible *thing to do, after all.*

Right. And have Hazel show up at her doorstep, discovering the truth that way? And then have Hazel humiliate her by telling everyone in Easton's class of '90 how irresponsible Pru had been in trying to foist off as true such an extensive lie about her life?

No, thank you.

So during their last few meetings—Pru hesitated to call them "dates"—they had embellished their story with all the proper details, and had rehearsed it repeatedly in an effort to ensure there would be no mistakes. On each of these occasions they had met at Pru's apartment. On each of these occasions Seth had spent as much time as possible with Tanner. On each of these occasions the two had strengthened their phony father-son bond.

Pru just wished she could say the same of their phony husband-wife bond. Unfortunately, on each of these occasions, she and Seth had, by silent and mutual agreement, kept their distance from each other. Sure, their stories were nice and pat—she had no fear that they would be caught in a lie there. No, what Pru feared now was that her body would be the weak link in the chain. Because her body simply could not remain unaffected by Seth's presence. Her body jumped, jived and wailed every time he came around.

And tonight, as she awaited his arrival at her home for yet another rehearsal, she felt no different in that regard. She sighed as she stared at the expensive, perfectly tailored leather luggage that looked so out of place in her living room. She was never going to be able to pull this off. Not just because she had no idea what went into living the kind of life she was pretending to have, but also because she simply was not comfortable whenever her alleged husband was around. Two people who were married and shared a child should at least *seem* to be comfortable together, she told herself. But whenever Seth came within twenty feet of her, she wanted to jump right out of her skin.

Right out of her skin and into his arms, she thought. Okay, so maybe she did have the right kind of reaction, to a point. A wife should definitely be turned on sexually by her husband. But that was just the problem. Seth *wasn't* her husband. Yet she was still completely turned on by him sexually.

Pru glanced down at her living room floor, where Tanner sat on his brightly colored quilt amid a vast and varied assortment of baby toys. "This is crazy," she said to her son. "*I'm* crazy. I can't believe I'm actually going to go through with this."

Tanner arched his eyebrows and drooled a little, but offered no other insight into her situation. Then again, she thought, drooling pretty much covered it.

"At least you and your father are getting along well," she said with a smile.

This much, at least, was true. Tanner and Seth had really

taken to each other over the past week, to the point where Pru sometimes thought her son preferred Seth's attention over her own. Then again, there was probably some sort of elusive, primal, guy thing going on there. Something Tanner had been missing in his life until now. He really did respond to Seth in a way he didn't with Pru.

She supposed she should be grateful. The fact was, though, there were times when she found herself feeling a little jealous. Not so much because of Tanner's preferences where Seth was concerned—she knew her son loved her unconditionally—but because of Seth's uninhibited reaction to Tanner. He gave so freely of himself to her son, didn't hold back a single emotional response. Whenever he was focusing on the baby, Seth was right there with him, laughing, playing, enjoying himself enormously. But the moment his gaze lit on Pru, she sensed an immediate and unmistakable withdrawal.

She had expected him to make another pass at her at some point over the past week. She had been prepared, every night they were together, to have to fight something off. And not just his advances where she was concerned, either. But her own advances toward him, as well. Because, Heaven help her, she wanted desperately to make advances when he was around. And it was with no small effort that she somehow prevented herself from acting on her impulses.

Thankfully, the door buzzer sounded then, something that kept her from having to explore more fully the troubling observations tumbling through her brain. She scooped up Tanner on her way to answer the door, and the moment she opened it to Seth, her son started kicking and flailing his arms about, laughing and cooing happily.

She was accustomed now to seeing him dressed in his off-duty duds, but the casual clothes still did nothing to diminish his air of authority and total confidence in his person. Tonight he wore more of those wonderfully form-fitting, faded jeans, and a pale-blue chambray shirt that served to magnify a hundredfold the blue of his eyes. Self-consciously, Pru smoothed a hand over her own pale-yellow shirt and blue jeans, hoping there were no lingering bits of sweet potatoes or blueberries dappling the garments.

"Hooray, Daddy's home," she muttered halfheartedly in greeting, extending the baby toward Seth without his even having to ask. It was, after all, a firmly placed part of their routine.

And, as he always did, the moment Seth entered the apartment, he tucked one hand under each of Tanner's arm-pits and lifted the baby high above his head. Tanner squealed with delight, kicked his legs like a frog and chat-tered incoherently. So Seth brought him back down, buried his face in the baby's neck and made a very noisy, slurpy raspberry against Tanner's throat. Tanner only laughed harder.

"God, I love this kid," Seth said as he held him at arm's length. "You've done amazingly well by him, Prudence."

She smiled. A bit perfunctorily, maybe, but still a smile nonetheless. "And hello to you, too," she said mildly.

He smiled back. A bit sheepishly. "I'm sorry," he told her. He leaned forward and brushed a chaste kiss over her cheek. "Hi. How was your day, dear?"

She shook her head, but couldn't quite work up any ir-ritation over his greeting. "Fine. The usual. Thanks for ask-ing."

But Seth had already moved into the living room with Tanner, had sat down on the couch and settled the baby on his lap, and now he was bouncing his legs on his toes to create a horsey kind of motion. "Trot-trot to market, to buy a loaf of bread..."

Tanner was beside himself with joy.

Pru just sighed.

"So what's on the agenda for tonight?" Seth asked after the ol' horse fell down *whoops* a few times.

"I don't know," she told him. "We've pretty much covered the lie that is our life."

Something in her voice must have betrayed her misgivings, because Seth glanced up at her with a curious expression. "You okay?" he asked.

She tried to shrug, couldn't quite manage it, so sighed deeply instead. "I guess."

"Still worried that we won't be able to pull it off?"

"Kind of."

"Prudence, we'll be fine. It's only for three days."

"I know."

"And we still have two weeks to go before we have to do our shtick."

"Yeah."

"So why are you worried?"

She lifted her shoulders and let them drop, but she said nothing to explain her fears. Mainly because she wasn't quite able to pinpoint what, exactly, she was so afraid of.

Tanner emitted a dissatisfied sound, so Seth went back to bouncing him on his lap. But even though he was looking at the baby, his words were directed at Pru this time. "Okay, so fill me in again on the whole weekend itinerary. If there are any weak links in the chain, we'll find them that way."

She moved to seat herself beside him and Tanner on the sofa, replaying the schedule in her head. "The Friday evening we arrive will be an informal reception with appetizers and a cash bar. It's supposed to be casual and unconstructed, so people can wander around looking for each other, exchange chitchat, get caught up, that sort of thing."

He nodded. "Ol' horse fall down…" he muttered playfully. Then, to Pru, "Okay. I don't foresee any problems there."

She had to agree. She figured the conversation at the reception would be of the most superficial variety, and since her entire life these days was superficial, then, by golly, she'd fit right in.

"On Saturday morning," she continued, "all of the social clubs will be meeting in different rooms. These are gatherings just for class members, not their families. I kind of wanted to go to the Spanish Club and Drama Club meetings. There are a few people I'd like to see."

"No problem," he said again, still bumping his knees up and down for the baby. "Tanner and I can keep busy while you do that. Right, kiddo?"

She bit her lip anxiously, still not sure how she felt about turning the two of them loose together. Certainly Seth *seemed* to know what he was doing, but Tanner could be a handful sometimes. "You sure you don't mind being alone with him?" she asked.

He smiled, but she couldn't help thinking that the gesture was meant more for the baby than it was for her. "Of course I don't mind. Tanner and I get along great." He stopped bouncing for a moment, then held a hand in front of the baby's face, and Tanner immediately curled his fat fingers around Seth's thumb.

"What about changing his diapers?" she said.

He shrugged off the question quite literally. "I've come a long way in that department. And I still have plenty of time to practice. It'll be a snap."

"You haven't changed any…poopy ones," she pointed out.

He paled a little at that, but quickly recovered. "Not to worry. It can't possibly be that bad."

Oh, if he only knew, she thought. "Just don't feed him any fresh kiwi," she cautioned.

His expression turned puzzled.

"Trust me," she told him.

"Hookay."

"Saturday afternoon is the picnic," she went on, swallowing the unsettling wave of nausea that uncurled in her belly. "All the families are invited. That will be a chance for everyone to meet everyone else's kids. There will be day care provided for all the other events, but children are de rigeur for this one. There will be family-oriented games and contests, three-legged races and stuff like that. We're all supposed to bring a basket meal to feed ourselves."

"Tanner and I will find a deli while we're out Saturday morning," he said, "and we'll get enough food to feed the three of us."

"Thanks."

"And then Saturday night?" he asked. Finally Seth lifted his gaze from Tanner to Pru, and when he did, his eyes were filled with speculation.

"That's the formal dance," she said. "Dinner, wine, live music, mirror ball, the whole nine yards."

For a moment he said nothing, only seemed to be lost in thought. Then finally he nodded. Slowly and with much doubt. "Dance," he repeated.

"Dance," she confirmed, feeling an odd uneasiness unwind in the pit of her stomach.

"Mmm," he said. It was a softly uttered sound, but one fraught with uncertainty.

"What?" she asked.

But he only shook his head slowly. "Nothing."

"No, you said, 'Mmm,'" she pointed out. "I want to know what you meant by that."

He lifted his shoulders again and let them drop. "Nothing," he repeated. "Just…you know…dancing."

She narrowed her eyes at him. "What about…you know…dancing?"

He shrugged again, but just as before, there was nothing

casual in the gesture. "It's just that the two of us have never…you know…danced together."

Uh-oh. "Are you telling me you don't know how to dance?"

He gaped at her, clearly outraged. "Of course I know how to dance. What kind of Dr. Irresistible would I be if I didn't know how to dance?"

She decided not to answer that one.

He blew out an impatient breath of air. "It's just that you and I have never danced *together,* that's all."

She eyed him suspiciously. "So?"

He rolled his eyes. "So, Prudence, every time I get within twenty feet of you, you get jumpy."

"I do not!"

He ignored her objection. "And I don't see how we're going to be able to dance convincingly if you're fidgeting all over the place while I'm trying to hold you."

"I do not fidget when you try to hold me." But she felt the heat of embarrassment warm her face as she formed the lie.

"How do you know?" he demanded. "It's been a while since I held you."

This time she was the one to gape. "It's been a while since you tried. I didn't know you wanted to hold me."

"Well that's a stupid thing to say."

"Seth!"

"Of *course* I want to hold you. Preferably while we're both naked."

"Seth!"

But again he ignored her objection. "I mean, what man wouldn't want to hold you—naked or otherwise?" He couldn't seem to help himself as he hastily added, "But especially naked?"

It was another question best left unanswered, she decided. Mainly because they could be there all night if she tried. "I don't see it being a problem," she said instead. "Number one, we won't be naked."

"Oh, I don't know about th—"

"And number two," she said, hurrying on, "I just think…" She sighed again. "I think we'll be fine."

"Maybe we should give it a practice run," he suggested. "The dancing, I mean," he quickly clarified, "not necessarily the holding. And certainly not the naked. Not unless you just want to, in which case I'd be happy to—"

"Oh, I don't think so," she quickly declined.

"What? The naked? The holding? Or the dancing?"

"All of the above."

He shook his head in obvious disappointment. "See? You are scared of me."

"I am not scared of you," she assured him.

"Oh, yes, you are scared of me."

"Oh, no, I'm not."

"Yes, you are."

"No, I'm not."

"Are, too."

"Am not."

"Prove it."

Well, that certainly shut her up. Prove it? *Prove it?* To Seth Mahoney? Oh…she didn't *think* so.

"I don't have to prove it," she said, sounding totally lame, even to her own ears. "It's not necessary."

He went back to bouncing the baby, but he continued to gaze at Pru. "Fine," he conceded. "It's not necessary. I just hope when Saturday night rolls around, you'll remember this and not get jumpy the minute I lay a finger on you."

"I do *not* get jumpy the minute you lay a—"

Without warning, and with great finesse, he lifted his hand and brushed his fingertips lightly, briefly over her cheek. Just one soft, quick stroke, totally innocent and without demand, but when it happened, instinctively, Pru jerked her head back from his touch. The entire episode lasted scarcely a second. Despite that, her heart hammered against her rib cage, her blood raced through her body, and heat shook her from her fingertips to her toes.

And Seth, damn him, had proved his point inarguably.

"Not jumpy," he repeated in response to her reaction. But there was something almost melancholy in his voice now that hadn't been there before. "Right."

Her heart still pounding, her breathing still ragged, she battled the urge to leap up from the couch and hide behind a chair. "I'll be fine," she said. "You just surprised me, that's all."

He smiled, but for some reason the gesture, like his voice, seemed a bit sad. "Funny, I could say the same thing about you," he replied softly.

She decided not to ask what he meant by his remark. She was probably better off not knowing.

But it was just as well, because he didn't wait for an answer, anyway. And he obviously had something else on his mind that needed saying. "After Tanner goes to bed tonight," he continued, "you and I are going to do something about this."

As rapidly as her heart had been beating before, it was nothing compared to the acceleration that occurred now. "Wh-what do you m-mean?" she stammered.

His gaze dropped to her mouth for a moment, then lifted back up to her eyes. Something dark and hot and hungry was burning there, and Pru began to feel a bit faint. Mainly because she suspected what she saw in his eyes was merely a reflection of what was simmering in her own.

"I mean," he said, "that this…this…this *thing*…that's been going on between the two of us…" He paused for a moment, as if giving great weight to some serious consideration. But his gaze never wavered from hers, nor did the fire and brimstone in his eyes cool even one degree. "Well, it's been going on long enough, that's all," he finally said. "And I think it's about time we did something about it."

"And wh-what exactly," she managed, "is it that's going on between the two of us?"

His smile turned knowing, and his gaze flashed with white-hot incandescence. "Oh, I think you already know the answer to that."

She shook her head, even though it was probably pointless to play dumb. Still, seeing as how she had no idea what to say, anyway, and seeing as how she wasn't sure her voice was even in working order anymore, remaining silent was probably the best recourse.

"I mean it, Prudence," he told her, his voice dropping in both volume and timbre. "No arguing. This thing going on between you and me? We're finally going to do something about it. Tonight."

"But—"

"Tonight, Prudence."

"But—"

"Tonight."

She swallowed hard, still unsure what to say. Her heart thumped wildly, her stomach somersaulted uproariously, and her libido tied itself into hot little knots. And somewhere deep inside, in some dark, impetuous place she'd never fully acknowledged, a deep-seated anticipation shook her.

Well, if you insist, she thought. Nevertheless, she felt totally unprepared for whatever he had in mind.

Seth, on the other hand, seemed totally unconcerned. Because his smile grew predatory as said with absolute conviction, "After Tanner goes to bed tonight, it'll be you and me. One on one. Just the two of us. Together, at last. Tonight, we're going to do it, Prudence,'' he vowed levelly. ''Tonight…we're going to dance.''

Nine

———

Dance? Pru thought. *Dance?* He was talking about *dancing?* Not…something else? But…but…but… That hadn't been what she'd had in mind *at all*.

The moment she recognized the inappropriateness of her expectations, she gave herself a mental smack upside the head. Hard. What was she *thinking?* That the two of them were going to go to bed together? That he'd been talking about having sex as a way to alleviate the tension between them? That he'd been suggesting the only way they'd feel comfortable together this weekend was to spend tonight rubbing up against each other naked?

Well, yeah, she realized. Basically that was exactly what she'd been thinking.

Now, of course, she felt ridiculous. Not just because of the absurdity of such a suggestion, and not just because she had misunderstood him so profoundly. But because in that dark, impetuous place deep inside her, she'd actually been

wanting to go along with him. She'd genuinely been looking forward to it. She'd honestly wanted him to seduce her.

Idiot, she chastised herself. Imbecile. *Irresponsible.* "Um, okay," she said. "We can do that."

Where before, the thought of being so close to Seth
would have made her edgy and uncomfortable, suddenly
she felt relieved by the suggestion. Dancing was a reasonably innocent way to alleviate her anxiety about physical
nearness. Maybe he was right. Maybe this was all that
would be needed for her to feel more comfortable being
around him. Maybe if they just danced together a few
times, she'd stop feeling so jumpy. Maybe that was all it
would take to appease this hunger that burned inside her.

And maybe a meteor the size of Rhode Island would
crash into the earth in the next five minutes.

"I'll give Tanner his bath now," she said, pushing the
thoughts away. "It's nearly bedtime, anyway. And then we
can…you know…dance. If that's what you want."

"Oh, Prudence," he said, his voice a warm caress that
seemed to stroke her entire body, "that's definitely what I
want."

In the long run, it was Seth who gave Tanner his bath,
Seth who taped a fresh diaper into place, Seth who wrestled
the baby's cotton sleeper onto his wiggling form. It was
Seth who fed Tanner his final bottle, Seth who read *Green
Eggs and Ham,* Seth who sang "Froggy Went a Courtin',"
and Seth who rocked the infant into a pleasant stupor before
settling him gently in his crib.

He was a natural, Pru thought as she watched him pull
Tanner's bedroom door to behind himself, leaving a few
cautious inches open. The man had a fathering instinct that
was obviously ingrained deeply into his DNA. Not many
men were that good with their own children, let alone
someone else's. Yet Seth Mahoney was a perfect candidate
for paternity.

Funny that he'd never married and had kids, she thought. It seemed that such men would just naturally be drawn into a family situation. He should be well settled into a life of wife and kids in a suburban landscape, yet he went out of his way to avoid that very thing. Why?

She had no idea, and she had a feeling that asking Seth would provide her with no answers whatsoever. He would simply shrug off the question as he did any query she posed that was of a personal nature. He'd toss off some flip, irreverent reply about wanting to save himself for someone special, then talk about how every woman was special in her own way. Never had Pru met a man who was so obviously one thing, yet went out of his way to assume the identity of someone else entirely.

Such an enigma. Such a gorgeous, charming, sexy enigma. Too bad trying to solve him would only lead to trouble.

"Got any Robert Cray in that CD collection of yours?" he asked as the two of them returned to the living room. "I'm kinda in the mood for blues tonight."

"Nope," she told him. "No Robert Cray."

"How about BB King?"

"Sorry."

"Okay, then. John Lee Hooker."

"Strike three," she replied.

He eyed her with obvious and grave disappointment. "What?" he asked. "You never sing the blues?"

She smiled. "Only when I'm drinking to forget."

Now his eyes narrowed with speculation. "And how often does that happen?"

She thought for a moment. "Not often. Not since...let's see now...not since Bobby Norris."

"Bobby Norris?"

She sighed wistfully. "I loved him so much."

Seth gaped at her. "You *loved* him?" he echoed incredulously, as if such a thing were unfathomable. "Seriously?"

"Oh, you bet," she told him dreamily. "I loved him with all my heart and soul."

He gaped again, as if her reaction were something completely alien to him. "No way."

"Way," she assured him. "Bobby was handsome and kind and sweet, and he had wonderful manners. Best of all, he wanted to be a lawyer when he grew up."

"Grew up?" Seth repeated. "Uh, just how long ago are we talking here, Prudence?"

"Second grade," she said, sighing again. "I must have gone through a gallon of lime Kool-Aid the day he moved to Paterson. It was so sad."

When she looked at Seth again, his expression had gone totally blank. Instead of commenting on the sad saga of Bobby Norris, he only made his way over to her CDs and muttered, "You must have something danceable in here somewhere. Slow dancing, I mean," he quickly qualified. "Not this Judas Priest stuff."

She pondered the question as she considered her collection. "There's some Barry Manilow in there, too," she told him. "The one with 'Mandy.'"

He swallowed a gag, then seemed to remember something, because he glanced over his shoulder at her and smiled. "Gershwin," he said. "We'll put that on again."

"That was a gift from my mother," she told him.

"Well, thank goodness someone in your family has some musical taste."

She ignored the remark and watched him rifle through her CDs until he found the one he wanted. After dropping his selection into the player, he pushed the forward button until he found "Our Love is Here to Stay." It was Pru's favorite song on the whole CD. Incomparably beautiful. Utterly romantic. Very, very slow.

She was in serious trouble.

As the first notes rippled out of the speakers on a drift of sweet piano, Seth spun around and opened his arms wide. "Dance with me," he said.

Knowing it would be pointless to say no—not because Seth would convince her otherwise, but because her traitorous heart would—Pru slowly moved toward him. She fumbled her nerve halfway across the room, however, and found herself hesitating over the last few steps. Naturally he noted her reluctance, and his shoulders slumped a bit in resignation as he dropped his hands back to his sides.

"Relax, Prudence," he told her. "All we're going to do is dance."

"I know," she replied. But somehow, deep down, she wasn't sure she really believed that.

"Then why aren't you comfortable around me? Why can't you come near me without feeling nervous?"

Oh, if he only knew, she thought. If he only knew she was halfway in love with him—and had been for some time. If he only knew she was getting closer to that destination with every moment she spent in his presence. She'd been too scared to admit it to herself, because there was nothing more irresponsible than falling for a man like him. Yet falling for Seth was exactly what she had been doing over the past two years. And now...

Now she feared there would be no turning back. Ever.

"I just..." She sighed fitfully. "I haven't been with anyone for a long time," she told him. "Not since Tanner's father."

He fastened his gaze on her face, his expression completely inscrutable. "It's been a year and a half since you've been with a man?" he asked.

She nodded. "Yes. You seem surprised."

He emitted a single, humorless chuckle. "That's because I *am* surprised."

"How can that surprise you?" she demanded. "How can you think I'd...I'd...I'd *do that*...with just anybody. Just because I'm a single mother doesn't mean I'm promiscuous."

"I never said it did," he replied evenly.

"I loved Kevin. Maybe not as much as I should have to become as intimately involved as I did, but I did love him. And for your information, there was only one other guy in my life before him. *Years* before him," she added. "And I loved that guy, too. Do you understand what I'm saying, Seth?"

He nodded slowly. "You're saying that you fall in love with the men you become sexually involved with."

She expelled a little sound of frustration. "No, that's not what I'm saying. I'm saying that in order for me to become sexually involved with a man, I have to love him first."

"And you seem to fall in love pretty easily."

She shook her head slowly. "No, I don't. That's just the point. And I need for you to understand that."

Neither his gaze nor his expression altered one whit. "I understand."

She dropped her own gaze to the floor. "And a baby changes things, Seth. Maybe not for all women, but it did for me. I don't want to go out with just any guy. Not that any guy is asking, anyway. That's beside the point," she hurried on. "Any man I go out with now, I'm going to be looking at him as a potential father for Tanner. I may not have had *very* high standards for myself before he was born. But you better believe it when I tell you that I have very high standards now."

"I believe you," he said softly.

"I'm not going to get involved with someone just because he's a nice guy," she added.

"I see."

"I'm not going to get involved with someone just because I find him attractive."

"I don't blame you."

"And I'm not going to get involved with someone just because I'm lonely."

He hesitated at that, his gaze growing deeper, more focused, more intense. "Are you lonely, Prudence?"

She sighed, wishing she hadn't said that. "Yes," she admitted nonetheless. "But that's no reason to…to…"

"To what?"

"To…dance…with the first guy who comes along and asks me."

He smiled, an enigmatic little smile that could have meant anything. But he said nothing, only opened his arms wide in invitation again. Unable to help herself, Pru laughed, an anxious little titter of sound that lingered uncomfortably between them.

"Come on," he cajoled softly. "You know you want to. I'm—almost—sure of it. It's only a dance," he repeated. "It doesn't have to be any more than that. Not unless you want it to be."

He really was irresistible, she thought. Funny how loving someone made them that way. She couldn't quite halt the smile that curled her lips, any more than she could keep herself from taking a step toward him. Then another. And another. Until finally she stood before him, barely an arm's length away. Seth covered that last step himself, then folded his arms around her.

He settled his hands on her hips with much familiarity, as if this were something the two of them did all the time. And although he pulled her body close to his, he didn't push his luck. With only a brief hesitation, Pru placed her open palms lightly against his chest, then slowly moved them upward to curl her fingers over his shoulders. As her hands grazed up along his chest, Seth sighed and closed his eyes, and he inched his body closer to hers.

There was nothing at all demanding in their posture, nothing even remotely sexual. A good two inches of air separated their chests, their hips only faintly and momentarily made contact. In spite of that, Pru felt as if her entire body were on fire. Something hot and urgent hummed just beneath the surface of her skin, held to a slow simmer for now, but all too volatile just the same. It wouldn't take much to push it to full boil, to wreak a spontaneous combustion of cataclysmic proportions.

Pru decided not to think about it for now.

Unfortunately, her body wasn't about to let her forget about it. Because every little move she made thrust higher her already acute awareness of the man before her. And every little move *he* made brought him slowly closer to her. And the closer he came, the more she wanted him. And the more she wanted him, the more difficult he became to resist.

As one song on the CD segued softly into another—"a Cloudy Day," she thought—he scooted his arms around her waist and hooked his fingers together at the small of her back. The action brought his body—finally—flush with hers, and he tipped his head to the side, rubbing his jaw over the crown of her head. Unable to help herself, Pru nudged one hand to his nape, curling her fingers over the warm skin she encountered. Then higher still, up into the soft strands of his hair, threading it through her fingers as if it were fine silk.

She felt him open one hand over the middle of her back, then he urged her body closer to his. She went willingly, her breasts pushing flat against his chest now, and she felt the rapid rhythm of his heartbeat echoing her own. Neither of them spoke, just continued to move in slow, lazy circles around her living room. But inside Pru a storm was brewing, thick with clouds to obscure her vision, rough with wind to chase away her reason, alive with lightning to alter the appearance of everything she'd always thought familiar. And only the hot rain she knew would follow would quench the demand of her needs.

As if he sensed the turmoil stirring inside her, Seth pressed his lips gently to her temple in a gesture that might have been soothing under different circumstances. The soft touch only inflamed her, however, made her want so much more. She clenched her fingers more tightly in his hair, then pushed the hand on his shoulder down over his back. He brushed his open mouth over her hair, his damp breath stirring the loose tresses on her forehead, wreaking havoc through her entire system.

Languidly she tipped her head back to look at him, only to find that his cheeks were stained with a flush of passion and that his pupils had dilated to nearly the edge of his pale blue irises. His lips were parted softly, as if he were having trouble getting enough air, and his chest rose and fell quickly in concordance.

Only then did she realize that the music had stopped, that their bodies had stopped, but that their hearts continued to pound with a rapid-fire staccato. And then she ceased to think at all, because Seth was lowering his head to hers, and she was pushing herself up on tiptoe to meet him. The moment his mouth covered hers, she knew that what she had suspected all along was true. She had fallen in love with Seth Mahoney. And she had no idea what she was going to do about it now.

Thank goodness she was so irresponsible, she thought. Because that gave her a really good excuse for why she shouldn't think too much about it. So she didn't think about it. She just reacted as instinct—as emotion—commanded her to do.

He looped his arms at the small of her back again, but

this time, instead of hooking his fingers together, he bunched the fabric of her shirt in both fists and began to free it from the waistband of her jeans. Pru didn't object, nor did she try to stop him, because she was far too focused on unfastening the buttons on his shirt. One by hasty one, she loosed them, then pushed the soft fabric open and buried her hands beneath it.

His chest was warm, vibrant satin beneath her fingertips, lightly dusted with pale-blond hair, faintly ridged with sturdy, poetic muscle. His torso was all hard planes and rigid bumps, so utterly different from her own body. Hungrily she explored him, sweeping her hands high and low, front and back, registering every last inch of him in her investigation.

Seth seemed as impatient as she, because he, too, was making fast work of her clothing. As she'd unbuttoned his shirt, he had freed the snap and zipper on her jeans, and now, none too slowly, he scooped his hands beneath the waistband of the denim, under the fragile cotton lace of her panties, until he could cup his palms over the bare flesh of her buttocks. He squeezed gently, and Pru caught her breath, propelling herself up on tiptoe when he increased the pressure. When she did, her pelvis made contact with his, and she felt him hard and ready against her belly.

As if even that intimate contact weren't enough, however, Seth rocked his hips forward, rubbing the solid length of himself against her. Pru's eyes fluttered closed, and she uttered a soft sound of surprise, of delight, of desire. So he did it again, pushing her forward this time as he thrust toward her, over and over again, mimicking through their clothes what he wanted to be doing to her naked.

"Oh," she said softly, her fingers convulsing into fists against his chest.

He withdrew one hand from her jeans, but splayed the fingers of the other open wide over her bottom. He settled one long finger in the delicate cleft bisecting her derriere, then pushed her toward his hard erection again as he wrapped the fingers of his free hand around her wrist. She paid no heed to what he was doing, until she realized he was pushing her hand lower, to the snap on his jeans.

Without having to be told, Pru opened it, lowering the zipper on a soft hiss of sound. Seth tightened his hold on her wrist, then tucked both of their hands inside his jeans, settling her palm over the head of his shaft, his palm over the back of her hand.

Together, they stroked him, deeply, leisurely, rhythmically, until his eyes closed and his lips parted and his breathing became ragged and clipped. He looked so wanton, so hungry, so needful, and Pru thrust herself up on her toes to cover his mouth with hers, kissing him hard as she clutched him tighter in her fist.

"Oh, Prudence," he said roughly as he broke off the kiss. "Oh, what you do to me. What *were* your parents thinking when they named you?"

Hastily he removed their hands and brought hers to his lips, trailing the tip of his tongue lightly over each of her fingers. When he got to her pinky, he sucked it inside his mouth, laving the sensitive flesh until she sighed her frustration. Removing it, he smiled shakily, and for the first time, she realized he was nowhere near as confident of himself as he let others believe. And the knowledge of that only made her love him more.

"So much for dancing," he murmured.

Pru said nothing, not quite trusting her voice or herself.

His eyes darkened as he focused on her mouth, and he said softly, "I want to make love to you." He returned his gaze to her eyes before adding, "Now. Here. If you'll let me."

She nodded, unable to respond with anything but agreement. "Yes," she said softly. "I want that, too."

He said nothing more, and she wondered if he was as worried as she was that speaking too much would lead to thinking too much. And that thinking too much would lead to doing too little.

She was about to turn toward the hall, toward her bedroom, but Seth tugged on her hand and led her to the couch instead, standing her in front of himself as he sat down. Immediately, he went to work on the buttons of her shirt, routinely loosing them one by one, a man with a definite mission.

"But—" she said.

"Now, Prudence," he repeated. "Here."

Instead of looking at her face, he was focused on her clothing, on tugging the worn denim down over her hips and pushing the soft shirt over her shoulders. The intensity in his eyes nearly stopped her heart, and without even thinking about what was to come next, she shoved aside his shirt and reached for his shoulders to steady herself. After shrugging the garment off completely, he pushed her jeans down to her ankles, and she stepped out of them, kicking them to the side, where they lay beside her own shirt, and his, on the floor.

Then she stood before him clad in only her panties and bra, gripping the hot steel of his shoulders for dear life. Instead of feeling vulnerable and inhibited, however, Pru felt surprisingly strong. The way he was looking at her made her feel powerful, almost omnipotent, as if, with one word, she could completely undo him as a man.

He settled each of his hands on the flair of her hips, stroking the pad of his thumb along her no-longer-flat belly. Then, without warning, without planning, without even asking permission, he leaned toward her and tasted her.

Tasted her. Completely. He dragged the flat of his tongue across the expanse of her bare belly, then dipped the tip into her navel before moving along on a new, upward path.

He moved one hand to deftly open the front clasp of her brassiere, then filled his palm with her breast. His other hand, too, began to move, taking a much more southerly route. Without fanfare Seth nudged apart her legs, tucking three fingers between them, then curled and uncurled them into the damp fabric of her panties, pressing the pad of each intimately against her sensitive flesh.

The breath left her lungs in a hot, ragged whoosh, and her knees threatened to buckle beneath her. Seth anticipated her, however, moving both hands back to her hips, but the moment she steadied herself, he skimmed his hands under her panties and pushed them down her legs. Obediently, Pru stepped out of them, only to find herself in Seth's possession again. He cupped his hands over her bare bottom, thrust her hips toward his mouth, and tasted her more intimately than ever before.

"Oh," she whispered wildly. "Oh, Seth..."

She told herself to object, to discourage what he so clearly intended to do, but the kiss of his hot breath against her damp, needy flesh halted the formation of any denial she might have been able to voice. And then his tongue...oh, his tongue...was there, too, rubbing in circles and straight lines, fast one minute, slow the next, at once languid and demanding, knowing and curious.

Never had she felt so close to the edge, so in need of satisfaction. She had no idea how long she stood there allowing his onslaught, needing his onslaught, only that it seemed to go on forever. And just as she was certain she would turn to hot liquid and spill over him, she sensed him moving away. After a moment, she found the energy to open her eyes, just in time to see him pulling her toward him again. Only now, he, too, was naked, heavy, swollen and hard, clearly eager to bury himself inside her.

"Get used to me, Prudence," he murmured thickly. "Get used to the way I feel, the way I taste, the way I touch you.

And get used to having me touch you—all over. Because I'm going to be all over you, sweetheart. And I'm not going anywhere.''

No, not tonight, anyway, she thought.

But she didn't have a chance to feel melancholy over the realization, because he quickly made good on his promise. His hands on her waist, he pulled her forward, and Pru knelt on the sofa cushion, straddling him. As she lowered her body onto his, he watched the union, his lips parting fractionally as he entered her slick canal. Inch by inch she absorbed him, his body stretching her, filling her, in a way she'd never been filled before. He was so… Oh. Perfect. So perfect. They fit together as easily as if they had never been apart.

When he was embedded inside her as far as he could be, Seth lifted his gaze to her face. His hair was damp and dark with his passion, his eyes were wanton and wild. He moved his hands to her breasts, covering them, lifting them, pushing them together. Then, still watching her face, he bent his head to fill his mouth with her, too.

Closing his eyes, he sucked her hard and deep, and, although she would have sworn it was impossible, she felt him swell to greater size inside her. His cheeks grew hollow with the pressure of his mouth, and she tangled her hands in his hair in a silent command for him to never stop.

As he feasted on her, he thrust his hips upward, and she squeezed her eyes shut at the keenness of the heat winding through her. Wanting to feel the full extent of his arousal, she rose up on her knees, then lowered herself over him again. This time Seth was the one to close his eyes and sigh, and the rush of his hot breath over her wet nipple jerked something inside her tighter still.

He moved his hands to her bottom again, lifting her higher and settling her down over him, again and again and again, the friction of their bodies sparking an inferno of need within her. Her breasts pushed against his chest, the soft bristle of his hair building fires along her already-feverish skin. Then, with one, swift, unexpected move, Pru was on her back beneath him, her legs wrapped around his waist, his entire body pushing into hers.

He was hard and heavy and hot atop her, and she could think of no other place she wanted to be. Wildly she bucked against him, and ferally he thrust her back down again. And just when she feared she would never again know contentment, the coil inside her sprang free, throwing sweet release to her body at the same moment the hot spill of his culmination sped into her.

His body went limp as hers did, and he rolled them awkwardly until they lay on their sides, her back pressed to his front, like two spoons in a drawer. A million things ran pell-mell through her mind, and she couldn't seem to fix on any one of them long enough to know what she was feeling. Behind her Seth's chest rose and fell as he tried to steady his breathing, but he cupped a hand possessively, almost lovingly, over her breast. She, in turn, closed her hand over his, but she had no idea what to say.

Seth's announcement, however, told her very well what he had on his mind.

"I didn't use a condom," he said softly. "You could get pregnant."

But he sounded almost…happy…about the realization, she marveled. Then again, in the afterglow of what they had just shared, she supposed it wasn't unusual for a man to be feeling pretty mellow and content, regardless of the long-term outcome.

"No, I won't," she told him. "I've been on the Pill since Tanner was three months old, to level off my hormones. Plus I'm only a few days away from my period. There's very little chance I'll get pregnant."

She wouldn't be lying here with him this way unless

she'd been confident from the start that she wouldn't get pregnant. She might be irresponsible, she thought, but she'd never make the same mistake twice. She didn't even trust condoms, since that was the method she and Kevin had been using when Tanner was conceived. And although she knew the pill wasn't 100 percent effective, she figured the odds still fell pretty well in her favor.

She had thought Seth would murmur his heartfelt relief at her revelation, but all he said was, "Oh."

And Pru told herself she must certainly be mistaken about the fact that he sounded so disappointed.

Ten

Now what?

As Seth lay stark naked on Prudence's couch—in more ways than one, he thought—that question, and that question alone, circled through his head. Circled through his head like a kamikaze fighter plane, just looking for the right place to go down in flames.

More questions quickly followed, though, and each was more troubling than the one before it. What on earth had possessed him to make love to Prudence? Hadn't she just told him, seconds before, that the only men she considered worthy these days were men she had in mind for husband and father material? In other words, *marriage* material? Hadn't she stated quite clearly that she could only have sex with a man she loved? So having just made love with Seth, did that not equate to her basically telling him she was in love with him? That she was weighing his assets on the marital scale?

Was she in love with him? he wondered. Or was it only that she *thought* she was in love with him? Was there a difference? And was she truly, honestly thinking about marriage? Marriage?

Marriage?

Too many questions, he thought. And not enough answers. He'd be especially grateful right now for an explanation as to why he had been almost disappointed—*disappointed,* for God's sake—to learn there was no chance that Prudence would get pregnant as a result of their... spontaneous combustion. Likewise, he'd love to know what he'd been thinking not to don one of the condoms he always carried in his wallet like a good Don Juan should.

Not that it seemed necessary to be wearing one now, but it sure as hell would have seemed essential had Prudence not been using some kind of protection herself. And he hadn't known *she* was using protection when *he'd* neglected to think about it. Ergo, why had he been so irresponsible in overlooking it?

More questions, he thought. And still no answers. He really did need to get out of here. That was the only way he would be able to clear his head enough to find an adequate explanation for his inappropriate, completely un-Seth-like behavior.

Then again, it wasn't the *behavior* that had been un-Seth-like, and it wasn't the behavior that was puzzling him right now. There was nothing unusual about him wanting to make love to a beautiful woman. No, what had Seth troubled so much now were the emotional repercussions of that behavior. Simply put, he'd never had emotional responses to his behavior before. None. Sex had always been a nice diversion, a sweet release of pent-up energy. A nice way for two consenting adults to pass the time.

With Prudence, however, sex had been a lot more than

a pastime and certainly more than a physical act. There had been feelings with Prudence, feelings *for* Prudence. Emotions. A response that was almost spiritual somehow. And Seth couldn't quite figure out what had been so different this time to generate such a reaction in him. More than anything, at the moment, he wanted to be alone, to try and figure out just what the hell he was thinking.

"Prudence?"

"Seth?"

They spoke as one and halted as one, and neither seemed to know what to say next. The way she spoke his name, however, so softly, so dreamily, as if she hadn't quite come back to earth, put something inside him on red alert.

She was going to invite him to spend the night, he thought. She was thinking about how nice it would be for the two of them to snuggle in the darkness, then wake up together in the morning. She was envisioning how the two of them—no, how the *three* of them—would share Saturday together tomorrow the way any other romantically involved couple—the way any *family*—would.

Somehow, Seth just knew she was going to turn over right now and smile a wistful little smile, then kiss him with much affection, then suggest they retire to her room. They'd make love again, maybe two more times, if he thought he could manage it—and naturally, he was confident that he could—then, fully sated, they'd fade into a deep sleep filled with erotic dreams. During the night she'd probably have to get up with Tanner at least once, and Seth would share yet another family ritual—the nighttime feeding. Then she'd return to bed, and he'd pull her close, and they'd sleep in each others arms until morning.

That was what Prudence was thinking about, he was sure. That was what she was going to ask for. So it came as no small surprise when, with her back still turned to him, she said, "I think it would be best if you went home now."

It was the perfect opening for him, just the one he needed, just the one that would allow him to escape without seeming to escape. *Oh, hey, I'd love to stay, Prudence, but since you've asked me to leave, I'll honor your wishes and…* It was what he wanted, after all—to be free of this awkward situation so that he could analyze the whole experience and figure out where he went wrong.

So he was even more surprised to hear himself respond, "So soon? But the night is still young."

"I have a busy weekend," she told him flatly. "I need to get up early in the morning. And I'm sure you have things to do, too. It would be best if you left now."

"I don't have anything going on that can't wait," he told her. "Nothing that can't be put off."

It was an odd exchange, to be sure, because they still lay spooned against each other, their legs tangled, her hand cupping his over her bare breast. Their pose was a lovers' pose, yet their conversation was anything but intimate. And although Seth told himself not to prolong what promised to be an uncomfortable parting, he found that he simply could not let things go that easily.

Stranger still, he didn't *want* to let them go that easily.

He pushed himself up on one elbow and rolled Prudence onto her back, so that he could see her face and she could see his. He had no idea what his expression might reveal—mainly because he had no idea what he was feeling or thinking at the moment—but hers was filled with confusion and uncertainty and something else he couldn't bring himself to consider.

In the pale light that spilled from the single lamp left burning, her fair skin was nearly luminous, and her green eyes shone like faint emeralds. Her dark hair was a riot of brief curls bunched against the pillow beneath her head, and it suddenly occurred to him that he would never get tired of looking at her this way. Never.

"What is it?" he asked. "Why do you want me to go after what we just...after what just happened between us?"

Her gaze held his for a scant moment and then skittered away to some point over his shoulder. "Isn't that what you want to do?" she asked softly. "Leave?"

Surprisingly, no, Seth realized. In spite of all the misgivings tumbling through his head, he had absolutely no desire to go. He genuinely wanted to stay here with her. All night, if she would let him. He wanted to make love to her again, wanted to hold her in his arms until morning, wanted to be the one to rise and give Tanner his nighttime feeding, if the baby would allow it. Seth wanted to awaken beside Prudence when the first fingers of light crept over the windowsill, and then he wanted to spend Saturday with her and her son, as a family would.

It was the most extraordinary thing to realize.

But not altogether unpleasant.

"What I want isn't the only thing at issue here," he told her, sidestepping, for now, the strange revelations coming to light in his brain. "What about what you want?"

She still didn't look at his face as she asked, "What about it?"

He inhaled a deep breath and released it slowly. "What we just talked about a little while ago...?" he began.

"Yes?"

"You mentioned...some things...that we probably need to discuss further."

Her gaze lit on his again, but she seemed more troubled than soothed by his words. "What I said then was just talking, Seth. Obviously I didn't mean any of it."

He ignored the little twist of pain that sliced through his chest at her comment. "Why do you say that?" he asked softly. "Why is it obvious?"

But she didn't answer, only shook her head mutely and glanced away once more.

"Prudence," he began again. But he lost steam some-where and couldn't quite make himself say the words he wanted to say: that he wished she would let him stay the night. That he wanted to spend the day with her and Tanner tomorrow. That they needed to talk more about what she had said a little while ago, about love and commitment and fatherly potential.

But the words got stuck in his throat and just wouldn't come. All he could manage was, "Do you really want me to go?"

She nodded, but still said nothing, still didn't meet his gaze.

"Truly, Prudence?"

Another nod. A long swallow. No eye contact whatso-ever.

"Look at me," he instructed her.

She hesitated only a moment before turning her head to meet his gaze full on.

"Now tell me you want me to go."

After another brief hesitation, she said, very softly, "I...I want you to...to go."

Seth, on the other hand, hesitated not at all before reply-ing, "I don't believe you."

She closed her eyes tight at his comment, and only then did he see the sheen of moisture on her lashes. "Seth, please," she whispered.

Unable to do anything else, he levered his body lightly over hers, belly to belly, chest to breasts. He settled himself between her legs, propping his weight on both elbows to cup her face in his hands. He didn't mean for the position to be sexual, and really, sex was the last thing he had on his mind. He only wanted to be close to Prudence, physi-cally, emotionally and every other way possible.

Gently he brushed the pad of each thumb over her damp

eyelashes. "You're crying," he murmured. "Why are you crying?"

She shook her head slowly, then wrapped both of her hands around his wrists in an effort to remove his hands from her face. "No, I'm not," she said.

He allowed her some success in her efforts, but didn't stop touching her completely. He threaded his fingers through the hair at her temples, then leaned down to brush a tentative kiss high on each cheek. "You are too crying, Prudence," he said. "And I want to know why."

She started to shake her head again, then seemed to think better of it and actually offered him a response. "Because I'm so damned irresponsible, that's why," she said. A single tear tumbled from one eye to punctuate the statement, and he quickly brushed it away with his thumb.

Still, he couldn't quite bite back the chuckle that erupted from somewhere deep inside him at her response. "You? Irresponsible?" he asked lightly. "Do tell."

Her eyebrows arrowed downward. Clearly, she didn't see the humor. He supposed, in a way, he didn't blame her. He wasn't sure he saw it himself.

"See?" she demanded. "You think so, too."

"No, I don't," he assured her. "Not about this, at least."

"How can you say that? I just…we just…and after I told you I could never…"

"That's exactly why," he interrupted her.

Confusion clouded her face. "I don't understand."

Seth sighed heavily. "Don't you?"

She shook her head slowly again. "No."

"Then let me stay the night, Prudence," he said impulsively. "Maybe together we can figure it out."

She gazed at him without speaking for a long time, her eyes fixed intently on his—so intently, in fact, that he could almost hear the little gears whirring inside her head as she gave thought to his request. Finally, quietly, she told him, "No."

That was all. Just…no. No explanation, no excuses, no clarification, not even a maybe next time. Just no.

It wasn't a word Seth liked to hear. But it was one he certainly respected.

"Fine," he said, rolling off her to sit on the edge of the sofa.

Immediately he reached for his clothing and began to dress. As he did, he noticed that Prudence reached for a ruby-colored throw that lay haphazardly over the back of the couch. She draped it over her shoulders and clutched it tight over her breasts, her head turned away as he clothed himself.

Seth had no idea what to say, what to do. Nothing like this had ever happened to him before. He'd never been asked to leave when he wanted to stay. And he'd never wanted to stay the way he did with Prudence. And not just for tonight, he suddenly realized. But for a long, long time to come.

He really did need to get out of there. But oh, God, how he wanted to stay.

Hastily he stuffed his shirt into his jeans and fastened them, then stepped into his shoes without bothering to don his socks. He bent and scooped them up, stuffed them into his back pocket and spun around to face Prudence. She sat on the very edge of the sofa cushion as if prepared to bolt should he try to come near her. He ran his hands restlessly through his hair in an effort—fruitless, no doubt—to tame it, then dropped them to his hips.

"We will talk about this, Prudence. Make no mistake about that. I'm still your husband," he added, striving for a lightness he was nowhere close to feeling. "At least for another few weeks."

She shook her head, then tightened the throw more

snugly around herself as she stood to face him. "No, you're not," she said. "I'm giving you an annulment. Right now. We won't be going to the reunion. *I* won't be going to the reunion. It was a stupid idea to begin with."

A stupid idea, he echoed to himself. Yeah, maybe she was right. But which idea in particular was she talking about? he wondered.

"Fine," he replied. "No reunion. We still need to talk."

She sighed her resignation, and the gesture caused the throw to drop from one shoulder. Somehow Seth kept himself from leaning forward to taste the bare skin revealed beneath.

"I guess that's going to be unavoidable," she told him, oblivious to his desire. "I mean, we'll be seeing each other at work every day, after all."

"That's not what I meant, Prudence."

She swallowed hard and dropped her gaze to the floor. "Maybe not," she told him. "But it's what *I* meant."

He eyed her thoughtfully for a moment, trying to ignore the icy sensation that was creeping up from his belly. "You won't even talk about this?" he asked. "You won't even discuss what happened here tonight?"

"There's nothing to say."

"Oh, no?"

She shook her head. "I behaved irresponsibly. That's all there was to it. And, hey, there's nothing new in me being irresponsible, is there? It's my standard operating procedure."

He expelled a single, humorless chuckle. "You know, Prudence, if you'd just give yourself a chance, maybe you'd realize that you stopped behaving irresponsibly a long time ago."

She snapped her head up and eyed him warily. "What's that supposed to mean?"

But instead of answering, he continued, "If you gave

yourself a chance, maybe you'd realize that you're not the high school kid you used to be.''

She said nothing, only continued to study him with much suspicion.

''Maybe you'd realize that you don't make decisions based on impulse,'' he told her. ''You'd realize you make decisions based on what you want to do.''

More of the silent staring.

''Whether on a conscious or a subconscious level,'' he continued, feeling as though the endeavor was more and more pointless with every passing moment, ''what happened here tonight happened for some other reason than that you were behaving irresponsibly.''

''Did it? I disagree. I think I behaved very irresponsibly tonight. I don't think you realize what you're talking about, Seth.''

He shook his head. ''Ah, dammit. Just forget I said anything,'' he muttered.

And then, wishing he could do just that, he crossed to the front door to leave. But before he opened it, he spun around one final time. ''You know, you're half-right. One of us was being very irresponsible tonight. But you know what, Prudence? It wasn't you.''

Without awaiting a reply, he opened the front door and strode through it. And he tried not to slam it on his way out.

For the next week Pru did her best to avoid Seth Mahoney. Which actually proved to be not all that difficult to do, because Seth seemed intent on avoiding her, too. However, he evidently had no such desire to avoid seeing Tanner. This became clear to Pru when she went down to the hospital day care on her lunch break the Friday afternoon following her...interlude...with Seth, and found him and her son enjoying a lively game of find the sock monkey.

Tanner was sitting on a section of padded alphabet

squares, his red romper a bright splash of color against the pastel letters, and Seth was sitting on the floor before him, holding the sock monkey in question behind his back. Every few moments he'd pull it out from one side or another or he'd work it up under his white doctor jacket and pop it out from under one lapel. And Tanner, God love him, never quite figured it out, fell for it every time, squealing his utter delight at each discovery. And with every infant giggle he expelled, Seth would laugh, too, flashing that heart-stopping smile of his. And then he'd start the game all over again.

For a moment Pru only stood a ways off, watching the two of them, battling the warm, fuzzy sensation that pooled in her belly, swallowing the lump that tried to form in her throat. It was no secret at Seton that Seth Mahoney liked kids. He often visited the hospital nursery to observe the newborns, and the women who worked at the day care center knew him quite well. And Pru herself had observed firsthand what a natural he was with the younger set.

But she still marveled at how much a natural he was and still wondered why he hadn't indulged his fondness for kids by marrying and having a few of his own—heaven knew there were plenty of women who'd be willing to accommodate him in the wife and mother department. He probably hadn't, she answered her own question, because he simply couldn't commit himself to one woman, even if the result of that commitment would be a child.

Pru had thought that the main reason he'd spent so much time with Tanner at her apartment was only because he wanted the baby to be comfortable with him in their effort to make their marital charade succeed. But now that their charade was off, there was no reason for him to prolong any kind of relationship with her son. Yet here he was, visiting with Tanner, all the same.

"He's been here every day this week. I think that's a record, even for him."

Pru spun around at the comment, to find her friend Teresa, who was in charge of Seton's day care, smiling at the same scene Pru had been observing herself. Teresa was Pru's age, but they otherwise had little in common physically. Teresa was tall and slender, with a fall of naturally golden, naturally straight hair that many women would pay hundreds of dollars to have themselves. She had dark eyes and a year-round tan, and an utter confidence in herself that Pru envied.

"Dr. Mahoney, I mean," she said, nodding toward Seth and Tanner.

"He comes down here a lot, huh?" Pru asked.

Teresa nodded. "Oh, yeah. The kids love him. He knows some really cool stuff to do with surgical gloves."

Pru decided not to touch that comment with a ten-foot response.

"And every time he's shown up lately," the other woman continued, "Tanner has gone bananas. He absolutely adores Dr. Mahoney." She turned to look at Pru. "And Dr. Mahoney sure seems to like Tanner, too."

Pru sighed as she returned her gaze to the two men in her life. "Yeah, I know," she muttered.

Tanner was going to miss not having Seth around. Then again, she thought, with Seth visiting him all the time here at the nursery, that may not be a problem. Not for Tanner, at any rate. Pru wasn't sure how she felt about it herself. Having Seth prolong his friendship with her son meant that he would inescapably prolong his connection to her. There was no way Pru would deny Tanner the company of someone he obviously cared very much about. But at the same time it would be more than a little difficult to keep seeing Seth, feeling about him the way she felt, knowing he didn't return her love.

Because it was love she felt for him. There was no point in denying that any longer. She'd been kidding herself for a long time, thinking she was too responsible a person to fall for someone like him. In many ways she suspected she had fallen in love with him the day she'd met him. Because he had never been far from her thoughts.

If only he were capable of loving her the same way. But that, she knew, was asking too much. He just wasn't the kind of man to fall in love. He was Dr. Irresistible, after all. What woman would turn him down? And what man would commit himself to one woman, knowing he had that kind of effect on the opposite sex? Hoping for a solid future with him was like hoping to open the door to the Publisher's Clearinghouse guys on New Year's Day.

One in a billion. That's what Seth Mahoney was. And the odds of him returning her affections were pretty much the same.

As if she'd spoken the thought aloud, loud enough for him to hear, Seth's head snapped around, and his gaze met hers. She was totally unprepared for his scrutiny, totally unprepared for the sputter of heat that ignited in her belly as a result. She had been totally unprepared for *him,* she thought. And she supposed she would never quite get over him.

If only things could be different between them, she thought. If only he weren't the kind of man who went through women like cellophane, and if only she were a stable enough influence to make him change his ways and keep him in line. But she was irresponsible, and he was irrepressible, and there was no way that combination could create a successful relationship. One of them, at least, had to be reliable in order for things to work out.

His parting shot of a week ago still echoed at the back of her brain. *One of us was being very irresponsible tonight. But you know what, Prudence? It wasn't you.*

She still wasn't sure what he'd meant by that. Obviously that he had been the one who had been irresponsible that night, but she didn't understand how. Certainly they'd both been instrumental in letting things go too far. But she'd known from the start what kind of man he was, and she had been the one who had the most to lose. It was up to her to make sure things didn't get out of hand. Yet she had surrendered at the first sign of trouble.

She'd done that because she was totally irresponsible. Maybe Seth didn't understand that, but Pru did. And she couldn't risk having what had happened that night happen again. The only way to do that was to make sure she kept him at a distance. So at a distance he would remain.

Seth was still watching her, cautiously, curiously, but without any venom or malice. Tanner grabbed for the sock monkey, and Seth let him have it, then he rose and hefted the little guy into his arms. A dozen easy strides had him standing in front of Pru, close enough to touch if she'd wanted. And, of course, she did want. Very badly. Miraculously, however, she kept her hands to herself.

Still, so much for keeping him at a distance.

His blue eyes were smudged by faint purple crescents beneath each, and his mouth was bracketed by lines of stress and fatigue. His pale silky hair was a bit unkempt, as if he'd made it a habit this week to repeatedly rake his hands through it. All in all, he looked pretty much like Pru felt. And for some reason that heartened her a bit.

"We need to talk," he said without preamble.

Pru felt Teresa shift behind her, moving away. "Oh, I think I hear my mother calling. See you kids later."

Pru almost called her friend back, suddenly feeling the need for a tall, slender blonde to hide behind. Instead, she faced up to the tall, solid blonde standing before her—the one who cradled her son so easily against his broad chest, the one who had drool stains on his very expensive-looking silk tie, the one who had spurred such an explosive response inside her just a week before.

Pru swallowed hard. "A-about wh-what?" she stammered.

"About us."

Well, gee, nothing like getting right to the point, she thought. "I, uh…I think we, um…we said ev-everything we…we needed to say, um, last week." There. That hadn't been so hard, had it? Just a little anxiety punctuating nearly *every single word,* that was all. Sheesh.

"Funny," Seth countered, "but I'm of the opinion that what we said last week amounted to nothing at all."

"Well, of course, you're entitled to your opinion," Pru replied lamely.

He smiled enigmatically. "I have a few more. Wanna hear 'em?"

She could only imagine what they were. Of course, once she began imagining those, she began imagining other things, as well, so much so that her imagination began to run wild into territory she really had no business exploring in mixed company this way, so Pru quickly put on the brakes. "Seth, I don't think it's a good idea for us to—"

"Just come to my place tonight, Prudence," he hastily interjected, before she had a chance to decline. "You and Tanner both. You've carried this entire relationship until now—"

"It's not a relationship," she interrupted.

But he ignored her objection, continuing with "—and I think it's my turn to take on some of the weight." He smiled that puzzling smile again. "Let me see what it's like to do that for a change. I've never had the chance to learn."

His expression was so earnest, his eyes so alive, she couldn't find it in herself to turn him down just yet. "What do you mean?" she asked instead.

His smile turned hopeful. "Just come over tonight, okay? Around seven? And bring your appetite."

She hesitated to ask him exactly which appetite he was referring to, but he seemed to sense her ambivalence all the same.

"Yeah, that one, too," he told her, his eyes flashing with heat now. "Lamb for dinner. And for dessert—" he sighed "—well, dessert will be entirely up to you."

Eleven

Naturally when Seth had told Prudence that dessert was up to her, he'd had something other in mind than the square, white bakery box she held in both hands when he opened his front door to her some hours later. Yes, he'd been hoping for something sweet and rich and tasty—and preferably hot—but what he really wanted to have with Prudence couldn't possibly fit into a box that small. No, for what he had in mind, they were going to need something that was infinitely larger than that.

Oh, well, he thought. At least she had come. But she hadn't brought Tanner, he noted, and he wondered what to make of that.

"Where's the little guy?" he asked.

She looked a little nervous for some reason—well, Seth could pretty well figure out *what* reason—but her voice was steady as she replied, "He's with a sitter. My cousin Barbara's daughter. If you and I have…stuff to…to talk about—'' her gaze flickered to his as she said it, then skittered away to some point over his shoulder ''—then maybe it would be best if we didn't have Tanner as a distraction.''

"Tanner could never be a distraction," he said, smiling.

She chuckled, a genuine, heartfelt sound that made him smile. "You have no idea," she told him. "You can't possibly imagine what life is like with a baby. I can't remember the last time I *wasn't* distracted."

Seth hesitated only a moment before replying, "I can."

Her gaze shot back to his, her eyes widening in surprise—or perhaps something else—but he only stepped aside to gesture her in. She said nothing as she passed him, and she seemed intent on claiming a wide berth as she passed. He tried not to chuckle warmly with delight.

The day had been unusually pleasant for March, downright balmy, in fact, and she'd risen to the occasion by wearing a lightweight dress the color of sea foam. The color enhanced the green of her eyes and complemented the dark curls kissed with red and gold that framed her face. The dress flowed shapelessly past her knees, nearly to her ankles, but Seth recalled on his own, too well, the curves and swells, the dips and valleys that lay beneath. She'd donned a sweater in deference to the night's cool air, but her legs were bare.

All in all, he decided, the outfit afforded some promise of an interesting evening.

So far, however, dessert was looking to be whatever was in the box, and he made himself promise not to push for anything more. Tonight he would be responsible, he vowed, and would behave himself in a manner fit for a mature adult. Although not many people would believe it, Seth did know how to be mature. He'd been mature for much of his life.

Just not his adult life.

Tonight, however, he would tap that responsible vein

again, and he would see what developed as a result. Funny, but he was rather looking forward to getting in touch with that part of himself again. He'd had a nice run being immature and irresponsible, but now it was time to grow up. A man had to do what a man had to do, and Prudence Holloway was more than worth it.

"You look beautiful," he said as she swept by him on a faint scent of lavender.

She spun quickly around at his compliment, and for a moment a flash of uncertainty knit her features. But as quickly as it had developed, it unraveled again—a good sign, he decided—and she smiled.

"Thanks," she said. Her gaze swept him from head to toe and back again, and he saw something burning in her eyes that hadn't been there before. "You don't look so bad yourself."

He'd taken great care to appear casual, without being *too* casual, had opted for a pair of loose-fitting khaki trousers and a lightweight navy-blue sweater. He wanted to look cool and confident and responsible—and yes, irresistible, too—and he wanted to give Prudence the impression that he could be counted on to do the right thing.

Because tonight Seth was determined to do the right thing. He only hoped that she was as keen on the subject as he was himself. Deep down inside, however, he was convinced they were both on the same wavelength. He was positive she felt the same way he did. He wanted her. She wanted him. He was—almost—sure of it. Only this time the wanting would be for keeps.

And the keeping would be forever.

"So what did you bring?" he asked. "For dessert, I mean?"

She handed the box over to him, but when he went to remove the string tied around it, she smiled and said, "Ah, ah, ah. No peeking. It's a surprise."

He smiled back. "I love surprises."

Her smile fell some, and her eyes clouded a bit. "I'm not sure I do," she said softly.

He said nothing in response to that, only held her gaze in silence for a moment. Just as that moment began to grow awkward, however, the timer on the stove erupted, both of them starting visibly at the harsh, grating sound. Quickly Seth returned to the kitchen to switch it off and remove the lamb roast from the oven, dropping the bakery box on the counter as he reached for the oven door.

"It smells wonderful in here," Prudence said as she joined him in the kitchen.

"My own recipe," he told her. "Just enough Dijon mustard and rosemary to make it interesting."

She chuckled as she leaned back against the counter and crossed her arms over her midsection. Somehow the gesture seemed to be one of self-preservation, of self-defense, but Seth tried not to think about that. Instead he remembered how soft were the curls tumbling around her face, how fragrant was the skin that lay beneath her clothes, how warm was the heart that beat within. And he remembered how much he had come to love her.

"I had no idea you knew how to cook," she piped up, scattering his thoughts.

He settled the roast on top of the stove, then tucked the French bread in for a moment to heat. "I suspect there's quite a bit you don't know about me," he told her.

She dipped her head forward in acknowledgment. "I suspect you're right. You always evaded any personal questions I asked you."

He hesitated only a moment before telling her, "There was a reason for that."

She eyed him curiously. "Was there?"

He nodded. "Not a very good one, but there was a reason."

"Would you, by any chance, be willing to tell me what it is?"

"Maybe," he said cryptically. "Eventually. After dinner. Would you like to pour the wine?" he said hastily, when he saw her open her mouth to object.

Immediately she closed it again, something that frankly surprised him. Prudence following orders. Now there was an unusual development.

As she wrestled the cork out of a bottle of pinot noir, Seth put the finishing touches on everything. And after filling the two glasses he'd left on the counter earlier, she handed one to him, then sipped her own and stared out at his condo with much interest. He followed her gaze, taking in the assortment of formal, elegant furnishings, trying to view them as a stranger might. Colors ran toward the dark—forest-greens, deep-blues, mahogany wood and ox-blood leather. The furniture was boxy and masculine.

He liked the place well enough, he supposed, but it completely lacked the warmth and lived-in look that Prudence's apartment claimed. Nor did his own dwelling offer any of the personal touches hers had. There were no photographs of relatives and friends, no casually thrown-about toys, no books lying spine up to hold their place.

Seth spent little time here, and it showed. And the reason he spent little time here, of course, was because it wasn't particularly homey or inviting. Not that anyplace really was, he thought further. Well, except maybe for Prudence's place....

"You have a nice place," she said. "I like the way it's set up. Do your many talents extend to decorating, too?"

He shook his head. "No, that was done professionally. Knowledge of interior decoration wasn't vital for my survival when I was a child," he added. "Eating was. Hence, I learned to cook, but not how to arrange furniture."

She said nothing in response to that, only turned to eye him quizzically as she lifted her wine to her lips again.

"I'm a fairly decent seamstress, too," he confessed, twirling his own glass by the stem. "Not that I can whip up my own wardrobe, but I can sew buttons and mend tears better than just about anyone. I can keep a growing boy in one set of clothes for two full years if need be."

Again Prudence said nothing, just continued to study him with much interest. So Seth continued, thinking she'd figure it out soon enough.

"I also know how to squeeze a penny until it bleeds nickels," he told her. "And when it does come to cooking, I can make a can of tuna fish and a box of macaroni last for a week."

Prudence set her wine on the counter with a faint *chink,* then traced her finger around the circular base and avoided Seth's gaze. "You were poor when you grew up, weren't you?"

"Poor," he echoed hollowly. He turned his gaze to his glass, staring down at the ruby depths, because he wasn't sure he wanted to see Prudence's reaction when he told her all the things he needed to tell her. "Not exactly poor," he said. "Poor makes it sound like we struggled to make ends meet. In fact, Prudence, my mother and I went to bed hungry more often than not. We seldom had ends to make meet."

She said nothing for a moment, then asked, very quietly, "Where was your father?"

Seth hesitated not at all before replying, "I don't know."

"But your mother was there for you, wasn't she?" Doubt etched the question, along with a faint surprise.

Still gazing down into his wine, Seth said, "Although I generally knew where she was, I didn't see much of her. She worked two jobs and socked away nearly every cent that she could, so that I would have a college fund. Even though, at the time, I thought something like, oh, say… *food*…might be a better financial investment, I'm grateful to her for what she did.''

''I thought you were the boy wonder who went to college on an academic scholarship.''

''Partial scholarship,'' he corrected her. ''I still had expenses. And trust me, although my mother's savings helped out a lot, it was still touch and go from time to time. There were, shall we say, extenuating circumstances.''

He did glance back up then, only to find that Prudence had dropped her gaze down to her glass. ''I'm sorry, Seth,'' she said. ''I had no idea.''

''Of course you didn't. How could you? It's not something I talk about to anyone.'' He sighed softly. ''But it goes a long way toward explaining why I am the way I am.''

She glanced up at him then, her eyes reflecting her curiosity. ''What do you mean?''

Instead of answering her right away, he turned his attention to the rest of their dinner, lifting the lids on simmering pots, switching off the oven, searching for a box of matches to light the candles on the table.

He tried to pretend his focus was on each of these tasks as he responded to her question, but what was really tumbling through his mind were memories he would just as soon forget. Unfortunately they were memories of what had shaped him as a human being, and he knew he would never be able to completely banish them, any more than he would be able to change who, essentially, he was.

''My childhood,'' he began, ''was notoriously unchildlike. From the moment I can remember being old enough to do it, I was taking care of myself. I never knew my father. My mother worked many, many hours a week. When I was extremely young, she took me to work with her. I colored the cast-off newspapers in the homes she cleaned until I was old enough to help her with the cleaning itself. As soon as I was of legal age, I got a job of my own."

Suddenly restless, he took the box of matches into the dining area and went about lighting the candles in the middle of the table. "But as I said," he continued as he did so, "what money didn't go to cover our rent—in an incredibly shabby studio apartment—or our food, went into a bank account for my college. My mother was determined that I would be a doctor. Not because I necessarily showed any proficiency for such a thing, but because she wanted to be sure I would always have a job, and that I would always be able to take care of myself. She figured the world would always need physicians."

Prudence seemed to sense his restlessness, because she picked up both their glasses and brought them to the dining area, placing one on the table before Seth. She sat down in the chair next to that place, a silent invitation that he should join her before continuing with his story. Instead of doing so, he picked up his glass and moved into the living room. His appetite was suddenly gone, and he was suddenly less concerned that dinner be perfect.

"Taking care of myself, Prudence," he said as he turned around and gazed back at where she sat alone, "became my way of life from the very beginning. Where other children were coming home from school to play video games and ride their bikes, I was coming home to tidy the apartment and make dinner and taking care of myself. When I was older, after school I was going off to work, *then* coming home to tidy the apartment and make dinner and taking care of myself."

The next part of the story was difficult to discuss, so Seth sat down on the sofa before continuing. Prudence stayed where she was, whether because she sensed he needed his space, or because she needed distance from him herself, he couldn't have said. In any case, their physical separation allowed him to go on in as matter-of-fact a manner as he could manage.

"I was sixteen when my mother was diagnosed with cancer," he went on, his voice sounding casual where his thoughts and feelings were anything but. "I spent the next two years taking care of her, as well. The money in my college fund was gradually whittled down to almost nothing—it went to pay her medical expenses instead. So I ended up working more, to put myself through college after her death.

"Because after her death," he said, pushing aside those memories to focus on happier things, "I promised myself that I would become the doctor she had always wanted me to be. Fortunately, I did end up showing a proficiency for science and medicine. More important, I enjoyed my medical studies. Although there are those who would have you believe I breezed through my education, I assure you, that wasn't the case. I worked hard. I studied hard. I sacrificed a lot. And when I finished my residency, when I started working and making a good living, well…I decided to buy myself that childhood I'd never had."

He turned his attention to Prudence then, hoping to gauge her response to all that he had just revealed, hoping that she comprehended everything—*everything*—he was telling her, without him having to spell it out for her. And judging by the look on her face, Prudence did indeed understand. Most of it, anyway. He still hadn't dropped that final bombshell on her.

Rising from her seat at the table, she said softly, "You've always behaved like a child because you were never allowed to be a child until recently."

"Yes," he replied.

Leaving her wineglass where it sat, she began to slowly close the distance between them, step by step. And as she approached him, she added, "The reason you've been so…irrepressible…as an adult is because you were forced by circumstances to be so restrained in childhood.''

"Yes," he said. So far, so good, he thought further to himself.

She halted in front of him, seeming uncertain about her next step, her next move, her next analysis. So Seth decided to help her along. He set his wineglass on the table beside the couch, then reached for Prudence's hand instead. Tugging gently, he pulled her down to sit beside him, and took comfort in the fact that she did so willingly. But where he wanted to wrap his arms around her and hold her close, he hesitated, opting to twine the fingers of one of his hands with the fingers of one of hers.

"And the reason I've always avoided relationships, Prudence," he said quietly, "is simply because I've just never known how to manage them." He waited until her gaze met his before adding, "Not until lately."

She narrowed her eyes at him in puzzlement. "What do you mean?"

Unable to stand being this close to her without having her in his arms, Seth tightened his hold on her hand a bit and urged her to lean backward with him. The moment they were nestled against the cushion, he draped his free arm over the sofa's back, dropping his fingers to her shoulder to toy with the fabric of her dress. It was light and gauzy and soft, much like Prudence. The realization made him smile.

"Being with you and Tanner over the past couple of weeks," he said, "has made me realize what I've been missing. Hell, being with *you*," he quickly amended, "over the past couple of *years,* has made me realize what I've been missing."

She shook her head slowly. "How can you say that? You've been with dozens of women, just since coming to

Seton General. Doubtless there were dozens more before
that. How could I be any different from the rest of them?"

"Well, for one thing," he said, "there haven't been dozens of women. Not in the way you think. And for another
thing…" He sighed deeply, holding his breath as he
thought about how to say what he needed to say. Finally,
he told her, "You *are* different, Prudence. Don't you see?
You have been since that first day we met. I've dogged you
for two years now. Two years. Other women I've asked
out, if they've turned me down, I've just moved on. But I
haven't been able to do that with you. With you, I've always come back for more. You've always been—" he
grinned at her "—irresistible."

She opened her mouth to speak, but no words emerged.
Seth couldn't help but smile. She seemed to be working
very hard to make sense of what he was telling her, and he
was reluctant to interfere just yet. So he reached for an
errant curl that brushed her cheek, wrapping it around his
fingertip as she processed all the information he'd fed her
so far. Yet still she said nothing, still she seemed unable to
figure it all out.

So with another sigh he continued. "Even without…
without *dating* you…without *dancing* with you," he clarified with a smile he couldn't quite keep from being las-
civious, "I've always gravitated toward you. And these last
two weeks, spending more time with you, talking with you,
being with you…making love to you…"

Her cheeks grew hot at the mention, and the pulse at the
base of her throat leaped to life. Interesting that, seeing as
how Seth, too, felt his temperature rising, felt his blood
racing through his veins. My, my, my but they were in
sync. Perhaps dessert would be on the menu after all.

"Doing all those things with you," he went on, "just
made me realize I've been kidding myself for two years. I

love you, Prudence. I've loved you from the start. And I want to be with you.''

Her lips parted fractionally as she studied his face, as if she were scouring his features for some sign of affirmation there. ''You don't mean that,'' she said softly. But there was the merest, faintest trace of hope punctuating the statement, and Seth clung to that for all he was worth.

He expelled a single, humorless chuckle. ''Of course I mean that. I want to be with you. I love—''

''Don't,'' she objected before he could finish saying the words again. She lifted her hand and pressed her fingers lightly over his lips. ''Don't say what you don't mean.''

''I do mean it,'' he said against her fingers, putting every ounce of conviction he felt into that simple statement of fact. ''I love you.''

She shook her head, but dropped her hand back into her lap. ''You say that now, and maybe now it's even true. But it won't last, Seth. It never lasts with you.''

He laughed again, but this time the action was heartfelt. ''Don't you understand?'' he said again. ''It's already lasted two years, Prudence. Even with me denying it to myself, even with you fighting it every step of the way, even with both of us doing our best to dance around the truth... I've loved you for two years. I love you now. I will always love you.''

''Oh, Seth...''

This time it was her own mouth she covered with her fingers, as if she were trying to halt the flow of words that threatened. But in her eyes he saw a cloud of doubt, a flash of uncertainty. And he felt a storm begin to brew in his belly.

''You don't believe me,'' he said flatly.

She scrunched up her shoulders and let them drop. ''I don't know what to believe.''

''Then let me prove it to you,'' he said.

''How?''

"Marry me."

"What?"

"Marry me, Prudence. Be my wife. We can do it this weekend."

"What?"

"We can do it this weekend, and then next week we can go to your high school reunion as husband and wife."

"WHAT?"

He couldn't hold back his laughter at the expression on her face: a mix of disbelief, shock and hope. "This will be perfect," he told her. And it would be, too. He hadn't thought about it until now, but they still had time to get everything ironed out. "Marry me this weekend," he repeated. "Then we can go to Pittsburgh, and it won't be a charade. It won't be a big fat lie. I *will* be your husband. I *will* be Tanner's father. We will be living a life of marital bliss with nothing but blue skies ahead."

For a moment she only sat there staring at him as if he were a lunatic, her eyes wide, her mouth open, her face drained of color. Then, suddenly, a small hiccup of laughter escaped her.

It was a tiny, almost silent sound. But it spoke volumes. More than that, it made Seth smile.

"What about the big house in Cherry Hill?" she asked, battling a smile. "Won't that still be a lie?"

He shrugged. "We can tell everyone we're looking for a new place, because we expect our family to be growing soon. *That* won't be a lie." He suffered a momentary doubt. "Will it?"

"Growing out of four thousand square feet?" she asked incredulously, reminding him of the magnitude of their lie. But she hadn't—quite—contradicted him.

"It wouldn't be a lie," he insisted. "Because I do want our family to grow soon. Provided you do, too."

"Beyond *four thousand square feet?*" she asked again.

He laughed, the sound coming from deep inside him, and *God,* it felt *good.* But all he said was, "I'm game if you are."

She said nothing in response to that, only nibbled her lip thoughtfully as her cheeks grew pinker still. "What about the garden clubs and the volunteer work and the subscriptions to the arts?" she asked.

"They can all be taken care of with simple phone calls," Seth pointed out. "Consider it done."

"But—"

"Consider it done, Prudence," he reiterated. "All of it. I'll take care of it. I'm perfectly responsible, you know."

"What you are," she said, shaking her head slowly, as if trying to take it all in, "is out of your mind."

"Maybe so," he agreed, the warmth of contentment in his belly spreading throughout his body. "But you know what, Prudence? This feels like the first truly responsible, adult thing I've ever done in my life. It feels good," he assured her. "It feels right." He pulled her close and brushed his mouth lightly over hers, once, twice, three times, then pulled back again. "Marry me," he said.

But still she didn't say yes. She didn't say *no,* he took heart in realizing, but she didn't say yes, either. What she did say was, "I don't know, Seth. I have to think about it."

He nodded, but felt no worry. "That, of course, would be the responsible thing to do," he said.

Her expression changed then, and would have been the same had he just slapped her upside the head with a big wet fish. "What did you say?" she asked.

"I said that thinking about it would be the responsible thing to do," he repeated.

"That's what I thought you said." But still her expression indicated her befuddlement.

"And see, Prudence, that doesn't surprise me," he went

on, "the fact that you'd have to think about it. Because you've been the picture of responsibility, ever since I met you."

She shook her head, narrowing her eyes now in confusion. "I don't understand."

This was the part he'd been waiting for, the part he really needed for her to understand. "If you were truly irresponsible," he said, choosing his words carefully, "you would have gone out with me the first time I asked you. You would have jumped right into a pointless relationship with some childish, womanizing gigolo. Instead, you fought it, fought me, tooth and nail. You knew better than to take up with some ne'er-do-well Dr. Irresistible who would be lousy husband-and-father material."

"Yeah, instead I took up with a ne'er-do-well mechanic who was lousy husband-and-father material."

"So?"

She gaped at him. "So then I got knocked up by him and abandoned," she pointed out unnecessarily.

"You were using birth control when you got pregnant, right?" Seth asked. "It just failed on you, correct?"

She nodded.

"That was circumstance, Prudence, not irresponsibility. If you'd been irresponsible, you wouldn't have bothered with contraception at all."

"I was still abandoned."

"That shows that the baby's father was irresponsible, not you. You've struggled all this time to make sure Tanner has everything he needs. You've made him the focus of your life, Prudence. He's a happy, sweet little guy because of you. Because of the sacrifices you've made. Because you've worked so hard to do right by him. I wouldn't call that irresponsible. On the contrary."

Her eyes filled with tears suddenly, a development that shook Seth down to his core. He'd expected her to react in

a number of different ways, but this wasn't one he'd anticipated at all. "What?" he said. "What did I say to make
you cry?"

She shook her head quickly, an action that caused her
tears to tumble down her cheeks. Then she exhaled a long,
ragged breath…and launched herself right into his arms.
Instinctively Seth swept her up into his embrace, roping his
arms across her back, around her waist, knowing that, from
this day forward, he would never, ever let her go.

"I love you," she said, confirming his suspicions, the
words coming out in a rush, as if she hadn't intended to
say them. "You are so wonderful."

That was something Seth was in no way prepared to
contradict. *This* was the reaction he'd been hoping for. So
he dipped his head to hers, covered her mouth with his and
kissed her the way he had been longing to do all week.

Pru felt that kiss all the way to her toes. One thing about
Seth Mahoney, she thought faintly as her body caught fire,
he really was irresistible. She couldn't imagine what she'd
been thinking all this time when she'd resisted. So she
stopped. Resisting him. And gave herself over completely.

And in that ultimate moment of surrender, she found
total contentment. She did love Seth. She had probably
loved him since she'd first met him. She'd just been too
responsible a person to get involved with him until he'd
grown up.

Her thoughts began to turn muddled as she felt his mouth
move from her lips to her jaw to her neck. Where last week
he had been leisurely in his seduction, this time he seemed
less willing to go slow. Perhaps the passage of so much
time since their last joining was what spurred his immedi-
acy, perhaps it was the simple acknowledgment of their
love. Whatever the cause, whatever the reason, Pru succumbed eagerly. Threading the fingers of both hands

through his hair, she skimmed her lips over his temple as he dragged his open mouth along the side of her throat.

"I think dinner has probably gotten cold by now," she said a bit breathlessly.

He nuzzled the side of her neck. "What dinner?"

She chuckled low, moving a hand to his back, palming the firm muscles beneath the light fabric of his sweater. "That wonderful dinner you worked so hard on," she reminded him.

"Mmm," he murmured. He lifted his head from her neck and gazed down into her eyes. "Interesting. Because there's something else that seems to be heating up."

A delicious coil of anticipation slowly began to unwind inside her. "You know, I noticed that, too. And it's exactly what I've been craving."

"Is it now?"

She nodded.

He was about to say something more, then glanced around the room, noting their surroundings. "This really isn't the place for the kind of feast I have in mind," he said.

She eyed him with playful suspiciousness. "Are you by any chance thinking about the dining room table right now?"

His grin in response to that was downright salacious. "Although I do believe that suggestion holds a lot of promise, let's try something really kinky this time."

She arched her eyebrows in silent query.

But instead of answering, he stood, extending a hand toward her in invitation. Pru readily tucked her hand into his, and rose when he tugged her gently to her feet. She was about to ask him where they were going when he bent swiftly and claimed her mouth again. As he intensified the kiss, tasting her deeply, soundly, possessively, he hoisted her into his arms. She gasped, and he took advantage of her open mouth to plunder her more thoroughly still.

When he scooped her up, he hooked his arms beneath her dress, under her legs, and moved his hand to cup her fanny, as well. Still kissing her, he strode easily down the short hall to the room at the end, which turned out to be, not surprisingly, his bedroom. He kept kissing Pru as he laid her down on the bed, continued to kiss her as he stretched out beside her, never stopped kissing her as he began working her dress up over her legs, her thighs, her torso, her breasts.

He did halt his persistent seduction long enough to work the garment over her head, but he quickly cast it aside and returned to exactly what he'd been doing in the beginning—tasting her, teasing her, touching every inch of her body. As his mouth wreaked magic upon her entire system, his hand went wandering on its own. Deftly he loosed the front clasp of her bra, then he filled his palm with her ripe, heated flesh.

He rolled the taut peak between thumb and forefinger, then swiftly dipped his head to capture the tight button in his mouth. He sucked her deeply inside, then let his hand drift lower, over the soft swell of her belly, into and out of her navel, beneath the lacy silk of her panties. Pru knotted her fingers in his hair as he plundered the damp curls between her legs, plowing up and down, forward and back, inside and out. With one long finger, he penetrated her, and she sucked in a fevered breath. Then his mouth was following the same path his fingers had blazed, trailing a damp line of passion in its wake.

She raised her hips as he pulled her panties away, then he was back again, fingering her moist cleft as he buried his tongue in the sensitive folds of her flesh. Gradually Pru became paralyzed by the indolent ribbon of heat that uncurled inside her, and all she could do was grip fistfuls of his hair in her fingers and whisper petitions that he both cease his onslaught and never, ever, stop it.

She was over the edge before she even realized she was
standing at the precipice, her body shuddering with one
echo of ecstasy after another. Insensate with still wanting
him, however, she opened her eyes to demand more, only
to find him, as naked as she now, kneeling on the bed
before her. She reached for him, and he gripped each of
her thighs in one hand, pulling her toward him. She fairly
climbed his body as he drove himself deep inside her, until
she could hook her arms around his neck, her bare breasts
crushed against his naked chest. Their hearts pounded
against each other, with an identical and demanding
rhythm, and Pru rose on her own knees briefly before
thrusting back down onto Seth.

He ground out a feral, uncontrolled utterance of passion,
cupped one hand over her breast and the other over her hip.
"Again," he commanded her in a rough, primitive voice.
"Do that again."

Feeling power surge through her body and soul, Pru rose
on her knees again, then sheathed herself over him once
more, propelling him inside her, down to her core. Again
and again, she set the pace, controlled the depth, sparked
and banked the heat. And over and over, she both claimed
him and gave herself, until, at a fever pitch, they both cried
out their sweet release. Their slick bodies arched and
bucked against each other one final time, then both fell
sated and gasping onto the bed.

The moment he withdrew from her, Seth pulled Pru
close, folding his body over hers protectively, lovingly.
Their damp torsos clung as they wrapped each other in a
tangle of arms and legs, and their chests rose and fell as
each tried to steady their respiration. For a long time, neither spoke, neither moved. They only held each other close,
expressing their feelings without words. Then a faint kiss
here, a soft caress there, and slowly they stirred from the
tempestuous fog that surrounded them.

Pru was the first to speak, her voice soft and solicitous

in deference to the serenity surrounding them. "Okay, I've thought about it," she murmured.

Seth chuckled low beside her, then dragged a leisurely finger along her thigh. "About what?" he asked, his voice every bit as licentious as the motion of his hand.

As if he didn't know, Pru thought. "About marrying you," she told him.

She felt him shift his body a bit, and then he was propping his head on one elbow, gazing down at her with eyes as blue and infinite as the deepest sea. "And?" he asked softly. Something in his tone, however, suggested he already knew the answer to that one-word question.

Pru lifted a hand and fingered back a damp, dark-blond lock of hair that had fallen over his forehead. "I've decided that I should marry you," she said with a faint smile. "It would be the responsible thing to do."

He smiled back. "So it would."

She inhaled deeply, a satisfied, contented feeling filling her along with the nourishing breath. "I love you, Seth."

The finger on her thigh began that leisurely stroking again. "And I love you, Prudence," he stated with much conviction. "I love every impulsive, spontaneous, fun-loving bone in your body."

She feigned consternation. "Just the bones?"

He shook his head. "Everything else, too. Every last DNA strand, every last corpuscle. If you want, I can recite each and every part of your body that I love, as I give it a thorough going-over. I am a doctor, you know."

"Dr. Irresistible," she said with a smile. Then she rolled onto her back, lifting her hands to frame his face. "Give it your best shot," she said. "I'm especially interested in learning what those little bones in my feet are called."

And with a wicked little smile and a murmur of delight, Seth did exactly as she requested.

Epilogue

"**P**rudence Holloway Mahoney, *there* you are!"

Pru spun around at the sound of Hazel Dubrowski Debbit's voice, surprised that it had taken a full twenty minutes for the other woman to track her down at the welcome cocktail party. Boy, Hazel was slipping.

"Hi, Hazel," Pru replied, smoothing a hand down over the black velvet Donna Karan cocktail dress she had bought specifically for this occasion.

She noted that her old school chum was dragging along two other old school chums behind her. Pru recognized one of them right off the bat as Stacy Barrett, whom she'd always found to be *very* annoying. And she noted that the other woman was Cathy Jennings, whom she'd always found *almost* as annoying. Neither had changed much, save a few extra pounds on their frames, and a different sort of 'do on their heads. After exchanging greetings and pleasantries with the women, Hazel got right to the meat of the matter.

"Where's your husband?" she asked sweetly.

Pru lifted her left hand to her hair, ostensibly to feather back an errant curl, but flicking her diamond-encrusted wedding band their way in a manner that caught the light overhead juuust riiight. The gems did *not* go unnoticed, she saw with a smile. "Oh, he's around here somewhere," she said airily. "He never strays far. The poor man is utterly smitten by me. And Tanner, too, of course," she added.

As if conjured by the mention, Seth approached the group, looking incredibly dapper and sexy in his expertly tailored, charcoal suit. He'd accessorized it with his usual accouterments—a ruby silk necktie, onyx cufflinks and a paisley Snugli. Inside that Snugli, Tanner was sound asleep, oblivious to the murmur of voices and the clinking of highball glasses and the soft strains of a string quartet in the corner.

"Ah," Pru said, lifting a hand to catch his attention, even though he was already fully intent on her and making his way across the room. "There he is now, the darling."

He halted beside her, passing her a glass of champagne complete with strawberry at the bottom, then lifted his own cocktail—Johnnie Walker Black and water, she was sure; she did know her husband so well, after all—to his own lips. With his free hand, he cradled Tanner's bottom, even though the little guy was fully secure in the pouch that was buckled over his father's back. All three women noted the affectionate father-son pose, and all gazed at the two in total disbelief.

"Child care has been arranged, you know," Hazel said, nodding toward the sleeping baby. "If you'd like to leave Tanner there, I assure you he'll be perfectly fine."

Seth gazed down at his sleeping son. "Yeah, but I'd rather have Tanner here with us. He's no trouble."

All three women exchanged that same look of disbelief, then turned their attention to Pru.

"He's a wonderful father," she said unnecessarily. "He shares in Tanner's care fifty-fifty."

Seth nodded, his chest swelling proudly at his accomplishments. "Yeah, I even change the poopy ones," he said arrogantly.

The three women gaped.

"It's true," Pru told them. "He's an amazing guy, my husband."

Hazel seemed to remember herself then, and turned to more important matters—well, more important to Hazel, at any rate. "So tell us about this big, beautiful house of yours in Cherry Hill," she said.

Pru waved the comment off. "Oh, we're looking for a new place," she said. "One that will accommodate our growing family. We need more room to spread out." That was all certainly true, she knew. Neither her apartment nor Seth's condo was suitable for the three of them. They really did need more room. Not necessarily four thousand square feet, but... Hazel didn't need to know the specifics.

"You're going to grow beyond four thousand square feet?" Hazel asked, her disbelief right back front and center again.

Pru just smiled and hooked her arm through Seth's, then leaned her head affectionately on his shoulder and sipped her champagne. Before Hazel could press for more information, she added, "Did you know the opera will be performing *Otello* this season? I can't wait."

Hazel shook her head slowly, studying Pru and Seth as if she'd just discovered them frozen inside a prehistoric glacier. "Well, I must say," she said. "I halfway thought you were making up all that stuff about being married when I saw you last month. But Prudence Holloway, you are positively glowing. I never thought I'd see the day when you'd be this upstanding and responsible."

"Oh, Hazel, please," she said, straightening. But she

kept her arm entwined with Seth's. "I was never that irresponsible, and you know it. I was just impulsive. Spontaneous. Fun loving. All that stuff."

Pru knew she was laying it on a bit thick, but honestly, she was tired of the label she'd shouldered for so long. She wasn't irresponsible. She was just…irrepressible. Like her husband. Dr. Irresistible.

"Now if you'll excuse us," she said, "we have to go mingle. I have *so* much catching up to do."

And with that Pru spun on her heel, pulling her husband and son along with her. She really did have a lot of catching up to do this weekend. Just not with any of her old classmates. She was on her honeymoon, after all. She and Seth had hardly begun.

Chuckling low, she tucked herself into his side, snuggling close as he draped one arm over her shoulder and the other under Tanner. And she realized that no matter what happened to her in life, she had everything she needed right here.

And it was truly irresistible.

* * * * *

Multi-*New York Times* bestselling author

NORA ROBERTS

knew from the first how to capture readers' hearts.
Celebrate the 20th Anniversary of Silhouette Books
with this special 2-in-1 edition containing her fabulous
first book and the sensational sequel.

Coming in June

IRISH HEARTS

Adelia Cunnane's fiery temper sets proud, powerful horse
breeder Travis Grant's heart aflame and he resolves to
make this wild ***Irish Thoroughbred*** his own.

Erin McKinnon accepts wealthy Burke Logan's loveless
proposal, but can this ravishing ***Irish Rose*** win her
hard-hearted husband's love?

Also available in June from
Silhouette Special Edition (SSE #1328)

IRISH REBEL

In this brand-new sequel to ***Irish Thoroughbred***, Travis and
Adelia's innocent but strong-willed daughter Keeley discovers
love in the arms of a charming Irish rogue with a talent for
horses…and romance.

Silhouette®

Where love comes alive™

Visit Silhouette at www.eHarlequin.com   PSNORA

SILHOUETTE'S 20TH ANNIVERSARY CONTEST
OFFICIAL RULES
NO PURCHASE NECESSARY TO ENTER

1. To enter, follow directions published in the offer to which you are responding. Contest begins 1/1/00 and ends on 8/24/00 (the "Promotion Period"). Method of entry may vary. Mailed entries must be postmarked by 8/24/00, and received by 8/31/00.

2. During the Promotion Period, the Contest may be presented via the Internet. Entry via the Internet may be restricted to residents of certain geographic areas that are disclosed on the Web site. To enter via the Internet, if you are a resident of a geographic area in which Internet entry is permissible, follow the directions displayed on-line, including typing your essay of 100 words or fewer telling us "Where In The World Your Love Will Come Alive." On-line entries must be received by 11:59 p.m. Eastern Standard time on 8/24/00. Limit one e-mail entry per person, household and e-mail address per day, per presentation. If you are a resident of a geographic area in which entry via the Internet is permissible, you may, in lieu of submitting an entry on-line, enter by mail, by hand-printing your name, address, telephone number and contest number/name on an 8"x 11" plain piece of paper and telling us in 100 words or fewer "Where In The World Your Love Will Come Alive," and mailing via first-class mail to: Silhouette 20th Anniversary Contest, (in the U.S.) P.O. Box 9069, Buffalo, NY 14269-9069; (In Canada) P.O. Box 637, Fort Erie, Ontario, Canada L2A 5X3. Limit one 8"x 11" mailed entry per person, household and e-mail address per day. On-line and/or 8"x 11" mailed entries received from persons residing in geographic areas in which Internet entry is not permissible will be disqualified. No liability is assumed for lost, late, incomplete, inaccurate, nondelivered or misdirected mail, or misdirected e-mail, for technical, hardware or software failures of any kind, lost or unavailable network connection, or failed, incomplete, garbled or delayed computer transmission or any human error which may occur in the receipt or processing of the entries in the contest.

3. Essays will be judged by a panel of members of the Silhouette editorial and marketing staff based on the following criteria:

   Sincerity (believability, credibility)—50%

   Originality (freshness, creativity)—30%

   Aptness (appropriateness to contest ideas)—20%

   Purchase or acceptance of a product offer does not improve your chances of winning. In the event of a tie, duplicate prizes will be awarded.

4. All entries become the property of Harlequin Enterprises Ltd., and will not be returned. Winner will be determined no later than 10/31/00 and will be notified by mail. Grand Prize winner will be required to sign and return Affidavit of Eligibility within 15 days of receipt of notification. Noncompliance within the time period may result in disqualification and an alternative winner may be selected. All municipal, provincial, federal, state and local laws and regulations apply. Contest open only to residents of the U.S. and Canada who are 18 years of age or older, and is void wherever prohibited by law. Internet entry is restricted solely to residents of those geographical areas in which Internet entry is permissible. Employees of Torstar Corp., their affiliates, agents and members of their immediate families are not eligible. Taxes on the prizes are the sole responsibility of winners. Entry and acceptance of any prize offered constitutes permission to use winner's name, photograph or other likeness for the purposes of advertising, trade and promotion on behalf of Torstar Corp. without further compensation to the winner, unless prohibited by law. Torstar Corp and D.L. Blair, Inc., their parents, affiliates and subsidiaries, are not responsible for errors in printing or electronic presentation of contest or entries. In the event of printing or other errors which may result in unintended prize values or duplication of prizes, all affected contest materials or entries shall be null and void. If for any reason the Internet portion of the contest is not capable of running as planned, including infection by computer virus, bugs, tampering, unauthorized intervention, fraud, technical failures, or any other causes beyond the control of Torstar Corp. which corrupt or affect the administration, secrecy, fairness, integrity or proper conduct of the contest, Torstar Corp. reserves the right, at its sole discretion, to disqualify any individual who tampers with the entry process and to cancel, terminate, modify or suspend the contest or the Internet portion thereof. In the event of a dispute regarding an on-line entry, the entry will be deemed submitted by the authorized holder of the e-mail account submitted at the time of entry. Authorized account holder is defined as the natural person who is assigned to an e-mail address by an Internet access provider, on-line service provider or other organization that is responsible for arranging e-mail address for the domain associated with the submitted e-mail address.

5. Prizes: Grand Prize—a $10,000 vacation to anywhere in the world. Travelers (at least one must be 18 years of age or older) or parent or guardian if one traveler is a minor, must sign and return a Release of Liability prior to departure. Travel must be completed by December 31, 2001, and is subject to space and accommodations availability. Two hundred (200) Second Prizes—a two-book limited edition autographed collector set from one of the Silhouette Anniversary authors: Nora Roberts, Diana Palmer, Linda Howard or Annette Broadrick (value $10.00 each set). All prizes are valued in U.S. dollars.

6. For a list of winners (available after 10/31/00), send a self-addressed, stamped envelope to: Harlequin Silhouette 20th Anniversary Winners, P.O. Box 4200, Blair, NE 68009-4200.

Contest sponsored by Torstar Corp., P.O. Box 9042, Buffalo, NY 14269-9042.

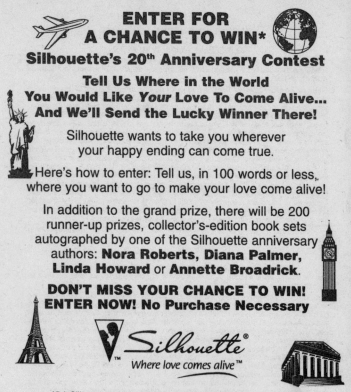

ENTER FOR A CHANCE TO WIN*

Silhouette's 20th Anniversary Contest

Tell Us Where in the World You Would Like *Your* Love To Come Alive... And We'll Send the Lucky Winner There!

Silhouette wants to take you wherever your happy ending can come true.

Here's how to enter: Tell us, in 100 words or less, where you want to go to make your love come alive!

In addition to the grand prize, there will be 200 runner-up prizes, collector's-edition book sets autographed by one of the Silhouette anniversary authors: **Nora Roberts, Diana Palmer, Linda Howard** or **Annette Broadrick.**

DON'T MISS YOUR CHANCE TO WIN! ENTER NOW! No Purchase Necessary

Silhouette®
Where love comes alive™

Visit Silhouette at www.eHarlequin.com to enter, starting this summer.

Name:

Address:

City: State/Province:

Zip/Postal Code:

Mail to Harlequin Books: **In the U.S.:** P.O. Box 9069, Buffalo, NY 14269-9069; **In Canada:** P.O. Box 637, Fort Erie, Ontario, L4A 5X3

*No purchase necessary—for contest details send a self-addressed stamped envelope to: Silhouette's 20th Anniversary Contest, P.O. Box 9069, Buffalo, NY, 14269-9069 (include contest name on self-addressed envelope). Residents of Washington and Vermont may omit postage. Open to Cdn. (excluding Quebec) and U.S. residents who are 18 or over. Void where prohibited. Contest ends August 31, 2000.

PS20CON_R2